LIGHT IN THE NIGHT

LE GRASSE Roger Pierre

Printed by: **Printing under contract with Amazon, Inc**

Legal Deposit: **September 2022**

ISBN: **978-2-493146-01-4**

Price: **$16.00**

LE GRASSE ROGER-PIERRE – 36 RUE DU MAGASIN – 45130 EPIEDS-EN-BEAUCE - FRANCE

DEDICATION

This story pays tribute to the women and men who, during the dark hours of the Second World War, showed humanity.
During this period, many people chose to fight against the occupier, and others on the other hand participated in the collaboration.
To people who had the courage to save lives at the risk of their own.
This book is dedicated to you.

TABLE OF CONTENTS

THANKS

To my family, to Stephanie Marie Hylard, to you who supported me in this project. Thank you for your support and unconditional help. To the women and men who sacrificed themselves in this dark period of our history to save people who were sometimes completely alien to them. To all of you, a very big thank you.

— Roger-Pierre LE GRASSE —

BEFORE THE STORY.

On May 10, 1940, the German army launched the Blitzkrieg of the Battle of France, which began with the invasion of Belgium, the Netherlands and Luxembourg.

Four days later, the Germanic troops managed to return to France by the city of Sedan.

On May 27, the Germans arrived in Calais. British and French troops retreat to Dunkirk. The Prime Minister of King George VI, Winston Churchill organized the most impressive evacuation of troops by mobilizing all types of boats.

On May 28, German troops surrounded British and French troops on the beaches of Dunkirk. The British troops with part of the French troops leave the continent.

On 16 June, Marshal Philippe Pétain, following his appointment as head of the French government by President Lebrun, contacted the Germans to request an armistice.

On June 17, Philippe Pétain announced the end of hostilities on the radio and loudspeakers in the cities and countryside. The newly appointed Brigadier General Charles De Gaulle, who took refuge in London, made his call to continue the fight on the airwaves of the B.B.C. on 18 June.

It was too late... The occupation had already begun.

Project: Light of the Night

1. THE BEGINNING.

Shortly after, the return of British and French troops from Dunkirk to England, the command of the British armies, under the influence of the King's Prime Minister, Winston Churchill, decided to train young British men, to gather information on the evolution of German troops on French territory. It is the Secretary of State of the War Office whose name is Anthony Eden, who gives the name of Project: light in the night to this secret operation. He would later declare that this name was to say that in the dark times of war, the glimmer of victory will dazzle the continent.

Anthony Eden was a Second Lieutenant in the Twenty-first Yeoman Rifles Battalion of the King Royal Rifle Corps. In addition, on June 3, 1917, he received the Military Cross for the Battle of the Somme. The Secretary of State, Anthony Eden, had planned and set up an organization and obtained from all the services of the State a total collaboration for the project light in the night.

The royal mail services were tasked with collecting information about people who are trying to correspond with a place in France. A special section in collaboration with the British intelligence service has been set up. Any mail to the France would be opened, read, and analyzed to find out if there are not messages to a suspicious person who may work for the German enemy. Police stations had been ordered to identify and monitor residents whose names sounded Germanic or Italian.

Personally, I love writing and I love France, since I was 10 years old. My parents with my brother and I go to a city to the south of this beautiful country called Bordeaux. I have friends there, in particular, my friend Marie Duval, I think

I have known her since I went on vacation in France. She taught me a lot of expression and vocabulary in French. And thanks to her, I am proud to say that I have a very good command of the language of this country.

Ah! I'm confused, forgive me, I didn't show up, my name is Lauren Elizabeth Cohan, I'm like you doubt now a young British woman. And I live near London. Finally to be more precise in a district of North London which is called Finchley. About Finchley, you could say it's the London countryside. It is very pleasant to live in Finchley. I love walking in the parks of our small town. Many people in particular, the French, tend to say that in the UK it rains all the time. And as I regularly tell my friend Marie, it doesn't rain that often in England. But it is true that this rumor is very tenacious. In fact, the other day, I sent a letter to my friend Marie. I hope she has received my letter. With the events, recent. I don't even know if she's okay. But in any case, I hope nothing happened to him. Well, I'm not here to tell you about my hometown. Let's continue my story.

It was a morning in August 1940, it was Saturday the 17th to be exact. I remember it like it was yesterday because Wednesday, August 21, is my mother's birthday. A man of medium height, about one meter seventy, who was dressed in a raincoat of light beige color. He had a gray suit and a black tie and hat like Humphrey Bogart in the movie "Invisible Stripes". He knocked on the door of my parents' house. My mother left to open the door for her.

— Mrs. Lauren Cohan?

— No, I am his mother.

— Excuse me, madam... Can I see your daughter please?

— What is the subject of your visit?

— Forgive me, I'm sorry. I did not show up. I am Second Lieutenant Nigel Billing.

— And why do you want to see my daughter?

— I'm sorry, madam, you will understand that I cannot talk to you about it on the landing of your door.

— Well, back.

— Thank you, madam.

The man entered our house. He pulled his black hat out of his head. I was standing at the top of the stairs. I had heard part of the conversation this individual had with my mother. I stared at him trying to find out what this man, whom I did not know, wanted me. My mother gestures to the man to enter our stay. Then seeing that I was at the top of the stairs, she motioned for me to come and say the words.

— Lauren, can you please come?

I had heard that the man said the name of a rank before saying his surname. Which I confess to you my many surprises. Why does a man with a rank want to see me? I am not a soldier, but a civilian. I had a certain fear. I began to go down the steps of the stairs that separate me from the ground floor of the house, one, by one and very slowly. Arriving on the landing of the ground floor, I took a deep breath, and I joined my mother who was waiting for me at the side of the stairs. My mother looked at me and said with her sweet and tender voice.

— There is a gentleman for you. He would like to talk to you.

I saw in the eyes of my tender mother that she was worried. I say to her in a low voice in order to reassure her.

— I promise you my dear little mother. I didn't do anything wrong.

I in turn enter the living room of the house. The man in a certain elegance stood in the middle of the room. He looked at me. I did the same. But I didn't see what this man wanted from me. Especially since, I didn't know him in the slightest. My mother asks the man to sit down. The man looks at my mother and gives her a smile. Then he delicately took a chair and sat down. He didn't take his eyes off me. He supports my gaze as a young woman who was looking for what this man wanted from her. The look of a young woman who is afraid and worried.

— You are Lauren Elizabeth Cohan!

— Indeed! That's my name. Can I know what you want from me?

— Don't be afraid. This letter... You were the one who wrote and posted.

He had taken out of his pocket an envelope that I had written to my friend Marie Duval. I recognized the envelope because there was a sign that we put on our envelopes to know that it was each other's.

— Yes sir... it is my envelope.

I was baffled. This man, whom I do not know at all, had one of my envelopes. Which suggests that he also had one of my letters with him. I do not understand what is going on. To confess, I was starting to get scared. What does this man want from me and why is he here? It scared me more and more.

— It was the Royale Mail that gave us your envelope and know, madam, that I have two others in my possession.

— What do you do with my letters? They are not for you! I'm not married so it's mademoiselle!

— OK... Miss it is not worth shouting at me. I only do my job. You may not know it, but the mail between the UK and the France no longer passes due to the war against the Germans.

— That is why I no longer receive mail from Mary.

— Probably.

— But you just want to give me back my letters! That's why you're here!

— Mademoiselle... You think Her Majesty's army is sending an officer to redistribute the mail not transmitted!

I look at my mother. The latter, staring at me and wondering what I had done as stupidity. So that an officer of the king's army came to our house on this day of Saturday, August 17, 1940, and to ask me questions about the letters I had written to my friend Marie. Marie Duval, this frail young woman, who lived in France. Did he think that my friend Marie Duval was a spy in the service of the Germans? Did he think I was a milking? My poor little mother, she must think to herself that I made a very big mistake for an officer to come to the house. What will my darling little dad say when he is that?

— But I didn't do anything! I swear to you, Mr. Officer!

— But I never told you that you did anything wrong! I have read your letters and that is my reason for being here.

— You have read my letters! It's rude! His letters are very personal!

— My daughter is right, it's not polite to read people's letters.

— But the law allows us to do so and there is a reason why we have read your correspondence.

— Oh, yes? Which one?

— All of them simply, it's that you write in France. On average, twice a month, according to the London Mail Delivery Centre. So this allows our service to read your mail to see if you are not communicating information about our troops to a person who would work for the Germans.

— That makes sense to me, my daughter.

— Mom! There are personal things that concern me, that Mary and me. I'm not a milking!

— Do not extrapolate what I have not said, mademoiselle. I never said you were a milking. I'm just saying that your profile caught our attention.

— How did my profile catch your attention?

— Well, you have knowledge of the French language. You could help England in its fight against the Germans.

— And how can I be useful to you?

The man smiled wide and answered.

— By working for us!

I was surprised by the answer this man gave me. I thought to myself how a 25-year-old woman could help the army. And why me? It's really strange and I don't understand why.

— How can you help my daughter? What could it do for you?

— We are creating a section whose function will be to collect information on the German troops in France. For this, we want people who have the ability to read, write and speak French.

I am not sure that my mother fully understood what the officer had just explained to us. She looked at this man, and then she looked at me. She says.

— My daughter will do herself an honor to help you Second Lieutenant!

I did not believe my ears; my mother had decided for me that I agreed to join the section of this officer. She made the decision without us being able to talk about it between us and especially with my little dad. It is very disconcerting; I can tell you. It was the very first time my mother decided, without us even talking about it among ourselves.

— Thank you, Madam, for your patriotism! I will come back tomorrow to pick up your daughter and her belongings. We have to go to our training camp in Kent.

— Oh! One minute! Mom your birthday is in four days. I want to be there with you to celebrate.

— Lauren, my sweet, and tender daughter, make me proud of your work to save the lives of our soldiers. Your brother, Isaac died before he could get on the ships that repatriate our troops from Dunkirk. Do it, in his memory, my daughter.

— Well mom, I would do it for Isaac.

The individual stands up. Then he walks to the door of the house. But before he leaves the living room, he turns to my mother and I and he says.

— Mrs. Cohan, thank you once again for your patriotism, it warms my heart, and I was sorry to learn that your son died in the fields of honors. Miss Cohan, I would pick you up tomorrow morning around 10 a.m. We have a lot of roads from here to Kent.

— Thank you, sir; my daughter will be ready when you arrive.

— Thank you again, Madam, for your welcome.

The man gets into a black car. It was rare to see someone driving a motor vehicle in our small town. He starts the traction and leaves in the direction of the main road which goes towards

London. In myself, I thought that it might be the last evening with my parents before long. So, I have to make this evening one of the most magnificent. I am sad that my brother Isaac is not present with us.

The next day, I woke up early. It must have been around 6:30 a.m. I wanted to enjoy my last moments with my parents. Because I couldn't know when I could see them again. I went down the stairs trying to make as little noise as possible. I didn't want to wake up my parents who are sleeping peacefully. I go to the kitchen to make a breakfast for my darling little mom and my darling little dad. I wanted to engrave in my mind their faces, their eyes, their smiles, and their voices.

My father and mother stood up. It must have been around 8:25 a.m., but to tell you the truth, I don't remember the time exactly. I was happy. I had managed to finish preparing breakfast for them. They came to the kitchen to have breakfast. The moment my parents walked into the room, I rushed in. I took them in my arms to give each of them a long hug. I didn't want them to realize how sad I was to leave. To have to leave them there. To leave several tens or even a hundred kilometers from them. After the long minutes of embrace, the three of us sat around our table. Then we had the meal together. I could see in my father's eyes the sadness of my departure. He was trying to hide it to prevent me from giving up. I would do everything to make my little mom and dad whom I love proud of me. Only, I don't know if my parents were proud of me at that time.

After breakfast, my little mom and I went up to my room to pack my suitcase. The difficulty this time, to prepare my suitcase, is that we did not know the duration of my absence. So with that we didn't know if I could come home for the winter to look for warm clothes. Personally, I wish with all my heart the opportunity to return before the end of August. But I am afraid that this is not possible. I thought I could send them my news by mail or leave them a message at our neighbor Clark's house. Our neighbor, Mr. Clark, had a phone at home. And in his great kindness, he allows the other inhabitants of our street to use his phone to make calls.

On the other hand, in my suitcase, I took care to put two important things to my heart. The photo of my father and mother and a photo of my brother and me. I miss my brother terribly. The ten o'clock approached at very high speed. You know, you must have already experienced it, or you tell yourself that you didn't have time to do everything you wanted to do or see all the people you wanted to see.

Ten o'clock rings at the bell tower of Finchley Church. A few minutes later, the black traction of Second Lieutenant Nigel Billing parked in front of my parents' house. The Second Lieutenant got out of the car and walked to our front door. I watched from the window of my room. I mentally prepared to go down and say goodbye to my parents. I think I'm saying goodbye because I intend to come back soon to see them. I hear the man knocking on our front door. This time, it is my father who opens the door. My father is a man who cares about respect for people of authority. Seeing Second Lieutenant Billing at the door of the house. My father took a step back.

— My respects, sir! I am Second Lieutenant Nigel Billing. I pick up your daughter Lauren Cohan to drive her to the camp in Kent.

— Hello, my name is Joseph Cohan. Please come in. I'll tell his mother to call him.

He said.

— Thank you very much, Mr. Cohan.

Second Lieutenant Nigel Billing entered our modest home for the second time. My father closed the door behind the man. The individual is placed on my father's right side. My father gave a slight smile. Then he called my mother.

— Ziva, can you call our Lauren?

— Immediately Joseph.

My mother climbs the stairs. As I told you, I knew that Second Lieutenant Nigel Billing was present in the house. I had already come out of my room. But as if paralyzed, I couldn't move forward. My mother gave me a wide smile. I have always been told that the eyes are like the door to the soul of the person. That some people could read in other people's eyes! Well, I can tell you that that day, I could see in the eyes of my sweet mother, the love she had for me. It was a bit like me at that time. Both loves, but also sadness. I had never really thought before that day. How much I will miss my parents! Then she said to me.

— My sweet and tender darling daughter. It's time! Pay tribute to your brother Isaac and make us proud. Despite my dear that you already make us proud of yourself. I want you to never forget that we love you and your father and me.

— My sweet mother... I too love you with all my heart. I am sad to abandon you.

My mother approached me. She gives me a sweet smile, takes my hand, and then kisses my forehead. I could smell its sweet scent of rose. Every morning, my beautiful and kind mom puts on the same brand of perfume she loves so much. You should know that the perfume of rose that my sweet and pretty mother puts it was as a result of a perfume that my wonderful darling dad had offered him on February 14, 1930. My mother, named it the perfume of Valentine's Day or the perfume of love. At the moment of my mother's gentle down, I couldn't help but make a slight smile. And know that even today, when I remember this moment of my life, I still have this little smile.

— Go, my daughter. Show them that we are strong.

— Promise Mom, I love you.

I head to the steps of our stairs. I go down looking at the Second Lieutenant who this time had put on his officer's uniform. I nodded at him, but I couldn't smile as usual when someone came home. It must be said that I had the impression that, my legs trembled by fear. It was as if someone was picking me up to drive me to the Tower of London. My heart began to accelerate. His beats were so loud that I had the impression that the people in the house could hear him. It was as if my heart wanted to come out of my chest to run away to hide. Second Lieutenant Billing looks at me and says in a soft, calm voice.

— Hello, Lauren! I hope you are doing well.

— Hello, sir, yes, I'm fine, thank you for worrying about it.

— Lauren, let me take your suitcase. We have to hurry; we have a very long road to the Kent camp.

— I could write to my parents to tell them where I am.

— Unfortunately, Lauren, I'll be honest, with you, correspondence and phone calls are forbidden where I'm driving you.

— So how am I going to give them my news?

— You will come back regularly. Rest assured!

— Lauren... Don't worry, my dear.

After his few words, my father gives me a tender kiss. It was on the do, and in the same place or, that my mother had kissed me on the screen. Then he said to me.

— Go, my Lauren, we are proud of you and do not forget that we love you.

I followed the Second Lieutenant. I get in the car. He started the traction. We left for Kent. During the journey, I look at the landscape from the window. Second Lieutenant Nigel Billing passed through London. I think it was to impress me and make me see that he knew well the streets of our splendid capital. We passed by the great old gentleman. You'll laugh, but I'll tell you one thing. The big old man as I say is the name I give to Big Ben. You know the great clock tower in London. We then cross the Thames. Then we drive to the south-west of England. We arrived near Ashford in the early evening. It was the first time I was going to be so far away from my parents. Be careful, I'm not saying I never left without my parents. I just want to say that I was usually no more than ten to twenty kilometers from them. And usually, I was with friends. He leads me into a building and in front of a door on the second floor, he gives me keys and tells me.

— Miss Cohan, here are the keys to your accommodation. Think, if you are resting well, tomorrow I will pick you up at nine o'clock to take you to the camp. Above all, don't tell anyone you're from the camp. You never know, there could be people sent by the Germans to spy on us. Good night.

He gave me the keys. I go back to this room. The room was sad. The colors were faded. I turn on the kerosene lamp. The room was equipped with a bed in metal structure. A table is placed along the wall with a wooden chair. A wardrobe with inside a wardrobe on one side. On the other side, several shelves. I started to store my clothes in the wardrobe. I hadn't brought much, subconsciously hoping to be able to go home the first weekend to see my parents. Once I'm done storing my stuff in the closet. I placed the two photographs of my father and mother and the other of my brother and me on the table which I think will be like a desk and in the evening, it becomes a table for the meal.

I sat on the corner of the bed. I started staring at the photos with some sadness. I think of my older brother Isaac. I think of his laughter. To tell you, my brother Isaac loves to laugh. He had fun making jokes to me all the time. You know jokes that aren't mean, but sometimes annoy you. But I loved hearing his laughter when he understood that I had fallen into his trap or prank. That night, I think back to many of his jokes. It's true at that time, I don't find them, at all funny, but think about it well his jokes were remarkably well organized. I was sad, but I was happy too. Happy to remember, his few moments, my life. A time when life's carelessness makes you not know if it's peace or war.

That night, I went to bed late. Which, believe me, is not my habit at all. I don't know if it's the fact that I was away from my parents or the fact that my older brother disappeared. I fell asleep above the blankets.

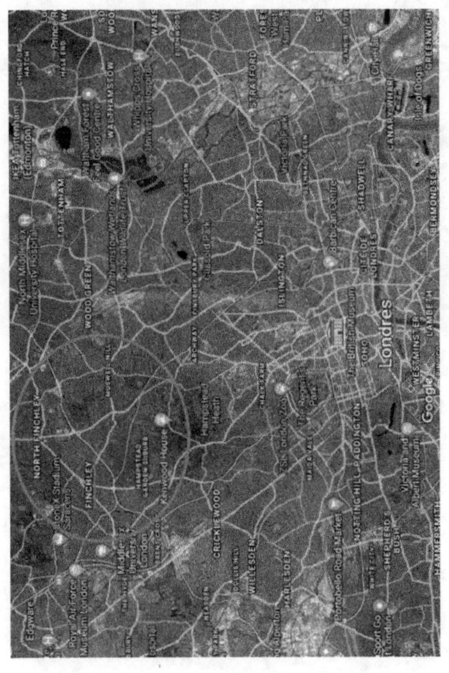

Map showing the city of Finchley in the suburbs of London.

2. TRAINING IN PAIN.

Nine o'clock sounded. It's been a while since I woke up. I had tea. I was particularly worried not knowing what awaited me during that first day. There was a knock on the door of my room. It took me a few moments before my brain reacted. I approach the door. Once positioned behind the door. I say.

— Yes, who is there?

— It's Second Lieutenant Nigel Billing! It's nine o'clock! I will wait for you by the car.

— No! I'm ready! ... I'm coming.

I open the door; the Second Lieutenant was there. He wears street clothes. If you prefer him, I mean he was not in his uniform like he was yesterday. He wears a black suit with a white shirt. He wears the same hat he had when he came to my parents' house for two days. We go down the steps of the stairs. And like all good Englishmen who respect each other, Second Lieutenant Billing went around the vehicle. And he opens the door for me to settle in. The traction starts and we drive for about ten minutes. We pass in a small town called Brook. At the exit of the small town, the Second Lieutenant turns on a small forest road. This small road was on the left about half a kilometer from the exit of the city. As we move forward, I feel like my heart is beating harder and harder. We arrive in a forest. The vehicle rushes into the wood following a path, which I think must have been felt. A little later, we arrive at a barrier. There were four soldiers standing guard. One of them walks towards us while the others surround the vehicle and aims at us with their weapons. I can tell you that I am starting to get scared. This is the first time a person has pointed a gun at me.

— Lieutenant! My respects! Can I see your pass and that of your companion please?

The Second Lieutenant took out of his inner pocket of his suit jacket a letter. Then he gives the letter to the soldier. The soldier looks at the letter and then he looks at Nigel Billing. Then he gives back to the Second Lieutenant. The latter again stores the missive in the inner pocket of his suit jacket. The soldier gave a statutory military salute. Subsequently, with his left hand he signals to a guard near the barrier to lift the barrier.

— Lieutenant... You can pass... Wishing you a good day.

We returned to the camp. The Second Lieutenant stopped the vehicle near a wooden building. To be honest, I had noticed that all the buildings in this camp were made of wood. I wonder if this military camp existed before the war began or if it was built shortly after. On each of the buildings of this military installation, there was a letter followed by a number! For us the building is the F4 building. To tell you the truth, even today, I do not know the meaning of the codification of the buildings inside Brook Camp. But I think this code had to be done for reasons of instruction. And that each of the buildings was assigned to a specific specialization. We entered the building and walked through a maze of corridors. Frankly, I felt like I was in a maze. If Second Lieutenant Nigel Billing wasn't with me at the time, I'm sure I would have gotten lost. And since we were in a military facility, I would have been arrested for espionage. The Second Lieutenant brought me into a room. This piece reminded me of a classroom like when I was younger at Finchley Girls' School. Nigel Billing turned to me and said.

— Lauren... Sit on a chair... another officer will come to see you.

— You don't stay with me.

There, I began to get scared. I said to myself, I don't understand. This Second Lieutenant asks me to follow him to lend a hand to our army and save the lives of our soldiers. And there, he informs me that it is not with him that I would do my instruction or that we would not work together. I thought the Second Lieutenant was going to stay with me. I was a little puzzled and taken aback.

— No Lauren... I have chosen you, so the procedure wishes that I cannot give you your instruction. That's the rule... Sorry... Don't be afraid, my colleagues are nice.

Second Lieutenant Nigel Billing came out of the room. I find myself alone in this very large room. As requested by the Second Lieutenant, I settled on one of the chairs. I noticed that there were about thirty chairs in the room. After a little while, which felt like an eternity, a man in uniform entered the room with a backrest under his arm. He stopped at the entrance of the room and looked at me. I wonder if this is the officer I have to meet. Suddenly, he walked directly towards me. He lifts a chair and turns it over, then he takes a seat on the chair. He puts the file he had on the desk, which is between us. Then he looked at me for a short while tilting his head slightly to his right side. But still without uttering any words. He had a pencil. I remember more than he having fun tapping it on the folder. After what seems like a long time to me, the man opened the file and said to me.

— You're Lauren Elizabeth Cohan. You were born on June 10, 1915, in London. Your father Joseph Isaac Cohan is an art dealer, and your mother is Ziva Elsa Cohan née Sterne. As for her, she is without a profession. You have a brother Isaac David who is your eldest and who has been missing since May 30 and the repatriation operation of our troops from Dunkirk. Is the information I just gave you, correct?

— Yes, sir.

— I am a Lieutenant. So you have to say... Yes, my Lieutenant.

— Sorry... My Lieutenant... I am not a person who has received military training. The only people in my family who have been trained in the military are my father and brother.

The Lieutenant looks at me and gives a slight smile. I think I must have told him something stupid. But to tell you all, I'm afraid to ask him. I do not wish to be ashamed. He tells me.

— Just kidding... You will have to be given a short course on the ranks and names of officers in the army.

— If that helps me.

The Lieutenant closes the file in front of him and utters the following words.

— Yes... I think that will be helpful to you. Now we must begin to teach you walrus, cartography, to recognize the various uniforms of the German army, the transmission of information. Because the sooner you are ready, the faster you can be entrusted with missions. Will you prepare it will be intensive.

— I'm ready, my Lieutenant!

— You see, you have already learned your first lesson.

During the last days of August and the first week of September of that year, the lieutenant's classes, of which I knew after two weeks his name, O'Connor was more than intensive. I wake up in the morning at six thirty o'clock. I arrive in the morning at eight o'clock at Brook's camp, I start with an hour and a half of combat sport. Then I enter the classroom for an hour and a half of mapping. Afterwards, I spend an hour learning message coding. I take a short break from noon to noon thirty. Then I resume starting with three and a half hours of walrus court. Followed by two hours of general sport. Then I continue with two hours of message coding and finally, up to twenty-two hours, it is to learn the various uniforms of the German troops. And this wonderful program is repeated from Monday to Friday, except that on Friday I finish at sunset. Indeed, they had taken note that I was of the Jewish faith. In my religion, Friday at sunset is called the Sabbath. We don't work.

On Thursday, September 5, 1940, Second Lieutenant Nigel Billing gave me the information that I would have a four-day leave to visit my parents starting on the weekend of September 14, 1940. But that for obvious security reasons, I shouldn't do anything, their sayings about my training at camp. I can tell you that I was extremely happy to hear this news. I believe that at that time, it was the most beautiful day of my life. I was joyful.

On Saturday, September 7, 1940, at about sixteen fifty-five o'clock, a terrible noise shook the walls of my room. I do not understand what is going on. I rush out of my room. Most of the inhabitants of the small building where I live have also come out. I guess from seeing people coming out of their homes that it's not just about my building. Looking at the ground, I see large black shadows passed. Like many people at that time, I began to look at Ashford's sky. And there, my amazement, I see many bombers and smaller planes passed over us. This squadron headed for London. A few minutes later, no more than two minutes, but what seems to me long at that time, soldiers arrived in town and asked the population with the help of the police to go to the cellars of the buildings. It was a real panic. Imagine parents running to shelters. Carrying their young children in their arms. The elderly as well as the police and military on the ground try as best, they can bring it to safety. I saw a group of men start running, jostling a pregnant woman and for some of them trampling her. A soldier helps the young woman get up and lures her to a building entrance. And in all this, the screams, and the tears. I worry and I ask.

— They are planes, friend, or foe.

— They are German planes and therefore enemies!

As requested by the authorities, I rushed to the basement of the building where I had taken up residence. The air attack sirens began to sound. I was scared. We can hear the hundreds of planes passing over us. Which I was even more afraid of for my parents. His planes are heading to London. I hope my little dad and mom will take cover. Children can be heard accompanied by their parents crying. The almost incessant noise of planes breaks a slight silence between two alerts.

The lights went out throughout the city. Sirens always emit their shrill noises. One begins to wonder if this was not the beginning of a ground attack by German troops. This lasted for a very long part of the night. It was around six o'clock in the morning, a soldier accompanied by a policeman entered the basement of my building to tell the people who were present that it was over and that we could go out. When I walked by the policeman who was present, I asked him.

— There is a lot of damage in the city!

— Not here madame... On the other hand... London and its suburbs, we suffer a lot of damage. There are, I think, a lot of deaths.

In his words, it was as if my legs had been cut off. As if one of the crew members of his planes was in front of me pierces my chest to remove my still beating heart. I broke down in tears thinking that maybe I can never see my parents again. Tears run down my face.

A few moments later, Second Lieutenant Billing and Lieutenant O'Connor arrive in front of my building. They saw me kneeling. They both came to meet me. I think his last ones were worried, and fear that I would be hurt.

— Lauren, are you okay? Ask Billing.

— London... Second Lieutenant... London...

— We know... We weren't ready. Say O'Connor.

— My parents? You know if my parents are... are...

— Unfortunately not... Sorry Lauren...

— Second Lieutenant... You will drive this young woman to her home in Finchley and see what can be done. You will give me a report on the state of London.

— At your command, my Lieutenant! ... Lauren came with me.

We left immediately. Second Lieutenant Billing rides as fast as possible. Besides, sometimes I admit that I had big fears. The journey was much longer than when we left my parents' house to go to Ashford. You will tell me that when we arrived a few kilometers before London we could see several columns of smoke. And we could also see, craters of bombs. What has some places, it gives an almost lunar vision of the London countryside. We had to be diverted from some roads because the piles of piles of stones of the buildings that litter the ground. This image of our beautiful capital made me sad. I can only think of the many people under the rubble. To his women, men, and children who on this beautiful day of Saturday, September 7, 1940, we had to go for a picnic, go out in the parks, for some eat in their gardens. This Attack by the Germans was dealt with because it did not target military installations, but only the population.

Arriving towards Finchley, and seeing that most of the buildings were destroyed, the Second Lieutenant said to me.

— Lauren... I will need you to guide me through the city. You have more knowledge of the terrain and the streets of the city than I do.

I guided the Second Lieutenant through the city until we turned down the street, or my parents resided. As we move forward, we see only houses in ruins. There were still a few houses still standing. But when the houses are not destroyed, they have suffered the very heavy damage. Then we arrived in front of my parents' house. There was nothing left of my childhood home. Goodbye my beautiful memories. I see neighbors rummaging through the rubble of my parents' house. One of them saw me and said.

— It's here! Lauren is here!

All of them stop digging into the rubble. The oldest son of our neighbor, John Clark told me.

— We were afraid that you were under the rubble.

— My parents are fine?

John turned to his father and then lowered his head. His father approached me and said.

— Lauren, I'm sorry... Nothing could be done for them. As soon as we went out, we came to the various rubble to look for survivors, but it was too late... We found them both... Hand in hand...

Then Mr. Clark points to a corner of the lawn. On this corner of the lawn, there was a white sheet covering my parents' bodies. I approached this sheet. I knelt down. And I wanted to lift that sheet to see my parents one last time. Second Lieutenant Nigel Billing followed me. The latter took my hand. And he said to me.

— Lauren, I'd be you I wouldn't. This can leave you with a bad image of your parents. The best you can do for them and in their memories is to keep in your mind the best memories you have spent with them.

I felt the world slip under my feet. I feel the tears flowing down my face. I admit it, I have a certain anger against the Germans. Because they attacked innocent people. It's not fair to my parents. Although I would never forgive his men for what they did that day! But it is also for the many civilian casualties. That day, I can tell you that I had a great hatred against the pilots of his German planes. I can say that I was somewhat anxious to face the German soldiers to take revenge for this infamy. As Prime Minister Winston Churchill said a few hours later.

I had a black look filled with hatred according to Second Lieutenant Billing. But how would you have reacted if people killed all your family members for no good reason? People who hadn't asked for anything. People who weren't even military. I look at Second Lieutenant Billing and tell him.

— We leave Second Lieutenant; I have nothing and no one here! The Germans will pay me!

The Second Lieutenant and I returned to Ashford without saying a single word. I just look at the bruised landscape of my beautiful and sweet country. It was as if my blood was in scree. If there had been a German in front of me at that time, I would have tortured him.

On Saturday afternoon, September 7, and during the night of Sunday, September 8, 1940, from seventeen o'clock to four o'clock, the Germans had sent three hundred and sixty-four bombers and five hundred and fifteen fighters to lower the morale of the British population. There were four hundred and thirty righteous deaths during this attack.

During the weeks and months that followed, I devoted myself to perfecting myself in cartography, walrus, close combat, the handling of weapons from knife to machine gun. I wanted only one thing. Kill Germans. I have only one thing left to learn. It's skydiving. The hardest part was that none of the instructors wanted to give me this instruction. I don't know if his people were misogynistic. Far be it from me to judge them. But every time I apply, I am told that I am not a priority. But I personally think that's also why I'm a woman. And that in the vision of men, a woman has the duty to stay at home to take care of the household and children. What I feel like sexism.

But hey, I'll wait for my time. I often went in the evening to a living room where men drink beer. But I personally drink tea and sometimes coffee. Although I find that coffee tastes bitter. It was one evening, it was mid-December, when I met a Colonel. I confess, I am very observant. And this Colonel had a badge on his uniform. It was that of the paratrooper forces. I approached him. And I ask to make a bet with the Colonel telling him that if I could take his military booklet, he would force an instructor to do the paratrooper training for me. It must be said that bets were frequent in the places of relaxation of the soldiers. Even if it was strictly prohibited by the Military Regulations. There were bets on all types of things. The Colonel agrees thinking that a frail young woman like me would have no chance of stealing his military booklet. Three minutes after our agreement, I told the Colonel.

— Colonel... Can you please show me your military booklet just to see how it is?

The Colonel replies with an affirmation that he still had his military booklet. Then he started looking for him. I confess that I let him look for him for a good two minutes before showing him that I had his military booklet in my hands. He was very surprised, and he told me.

— Bravo, you beat me... Know that I am a man of honor and so tomorrow morning you can go to Sergeant White for your training. Congratulations again.

— But it was a joy my Colonel!

Then I thought in my head.

Finally! With this new string to my bow, I would soon be ready for my revenge against his German assassins!

The next morning, I went to Sergeant White's section.

— My respects, Sergeant... I am sent by the Colonel...

— Oh yes... It was you who had stolen his military booklet...

— Uh... Technically, I didn't steal his military booklet... I borrowed from him so that I could follow your instruction.

— Yes, but he... He said you had stolen his military booklet!

— Well, that's wrong.

— It's mid-December... As you are a woman, I tell myself that at the end of March you will be ready.

— I promise you that I would be ready beforehand.

Training began. It was very hard especially since the men felt belittled to see me by their side. I admit it, I spent many dirty quarter-hours as they say. I felt like the training was harder for me than for my male colleagues. I held on, nothing will make me let go of my goal of taking revenge on the Germans in memory of my brother and my parents. As I told Sergeant White, I gave it my all. The section of the parachuting troops had set up a fake aircraft door, four meters high and mattresses at the feet to receive us without injuring us. When we arrived in the morning, Sergeant White made us run for three long hours. Then we had to do a small obstacle course. What the military calls an obstacle course. We had to learn how to climb the rope to touch a scarf that was placed six meters from the ground.

After two trying weeks, and believe me, this is no sinecure. Sergeant White informs the section in which I was the one and only woman that it is time to move on to the festivities. I can tell you for myself I would never understand if he had dared to call it rejoicing. I find that this term does not suit what I have experienced. The first few days, he put us on a plane set up to transport soldiers. And has an attitude of two feet, which gives a height of about sixty meters, he orders us to jump and that if a person refuses to jump, he removes the bag of parachutes and throws it through the opening. I approached the door of the plane. I take a deep breath and before I get ready to jump, I feel like I'm being pushed out of the plane. The following week, it was six hundred feet high, or approximately one hundred and eighty-two meters above sea level. But there, I did not let myself do it I started to run to the door and threw myself out of the plane. I finished my training session as fast as the men.

From now on, I can apply my revenge.

Second Lieutenant Billing and Lieutenant O'Connor came to see me to have completed my training. The Lieutenant had a file under his right arm, and they asked me to follow them. What I do wonders what is going on. I wonder if I had made a mistake. We head to the F6 building. It was the first time I entered this building. I follow them in the maze of corridors. The Lieutenant opens a door to a room and asks me to go back. I walk into the room. It wasn't like in the F4 building, it wasn't an instruction room. But a room with a model. And by observing the model that was placed on tripods. I recognized the region of my vacation. The Lieutenant said to me.

— Lauren, please sit down.

I sit on a chair and listen to it.

— We have a mission, and it is potentially dangerous. Well, you know how to speak French, that's why you were chosen. Do you know the Bordeaux region?

— Yes, I have my friend Marie Duval who is from Bordeaux.

— You are going to be parachuted over the Bordeaux region and you are going to transmit to us the German troop movements in this sector. Do you agree?

— Of course. When are we going to leave?

— Tonight. This is an important mission. We're counting on you Lauren.

— I will not disappoint you.

— You will be under the command of Second Lieutenant Billing. Will you prepare.

— Finally the departure for a mission.

A few hours later. Lauren, Second Lieutenant Billing and two other soldiers board the plane. Stress begins to rise in us. Finally me in any case, I was in a hurry to do this mission.

The plane took off and the flight will go well. Finally until anti-aircraft guns decided to shoot at us.

Sitemap of the city of Ashford.

3. FRANCE, HERE WE ARE!

It has been almost ten minutes since the anti-aircraft guns fired at us. The pilots of the plane try as best they can to avoid the shells of the German DCA. The plane oscillates in the air. As a result, we were tossed from left to right. One of the crew members comes up to us and tells us.

— I'm sorry, but you're going to have to jump now. We will not last long.

The Second Lieutenant replied.

— Are we far from our goal?

— Unfortunately yes. Several hundred kilometers, but I am unable to give you an accurate estimate. You have to jump.

— Damn! Okay, let us signal, when we can jump.

— At your command!

The Second Lieutenant stood up and motioned to us that we should also stand up. We were going to jump despite the German fire. We got up and walked towards the jump door of the plane. The difficulty was to stay upright despite the movements of the plane. Next to the door, a red headlight starts flashing. Then, it remained red as it stopped flashing. Then a green light came on. The Second Lieutenant began to scream.

— Come on, let's jump... We jump...

We rushed out of the plane. Around us, there were the explosions of the shells of the German anti-aircraft in France. It seems to me that the German troops do not appreciate the passage of our plane over the occupied territory of France.

But during my jump, I try to spot landmarks that I have identified on the model. But it was strange I don't recognize anything. Yet for 1 hour I had observed this model. I don't understand why I can't find my landmarks. After a few minutes of descent, I finally touch French soil. Suddenly, a stronger explosion than the previous ones was heard. The plane that transported us has just been hit by one of the shells of the German DCA. The plane descended in a flaming torch like a meteorite on fire as it entered the Earth's atmosphere.

I couldn't see if the crew members of the plane had time to rush out of the plane before the German anti-aircraft shell hit the plane.

I started looking for Second Lieutenant Billing and the other two members of our team. We had jumped over a small forest. After five minutes of searching, I came across the inert body of a member of our team. The poor man had to break his neck clinging to a branch of a tree. A few moments later, I am joined by the Second Lieutenant and the second soldier of our team.

With the help of the second soldier and Second Lieutenant Billing, we managed to detach our colleague's body from the tree. It is placed on the floor of the small wood. The second soldier begins to dig a hole to bury our comrade-in-arms. Second Lieutenant Nigel Billing looks at him and tells him.

— Soldier, I'm not sure we have time to bury our comrade.

— But my Lieutenant, we cannot leave him like that.

— I'm sorry soldier. But that would be too dangerous. Second Lieutenant Billing replied.

At the end of this sentence pronounced by the Second Lieutenant, we hear in the distance dog barking. I look at the Second Lieutenant and tell him.

— My Lieutenant... During the jump, I tried to spot our position in the Bordeaux sector, but I did not recognize the sector. I cannot tell you if the crew of the plane managed to jump before the plane crashed to the ground.

— How do you tell you Lauren? We are a few hundred kilometers from our goal. It was the co-pilot of the plane who confirmed this to me before asking us to jump off the plane. Right now, I confess that I do not know, where we are in France.

Second Lieutenant Billing looked around and saw a glimmer in the distance. It was the glow of a farm. A secluded house a few distances from our position. Lauren says.

— Let's go to this farm, Second Lieutenant.

— No because the Germans will automatically search in places close to our parachute drop.

The small group of three British commandos set out for a more distant commune. We moved and walked for about three quarters of an hour. While we were walking, Second Lieutenant Billing stepped into a hole which meant that he sprained his left ankle. We saw light in a house near the train station in the city of Meung-sur-Loire. The soldier who was with us climbed the small wall that determines the perimeter of the property. The shutters of the house were open. He was able to observe inside the house and lives a woman with her child of about five years. He watched them for several minutes to find out if other people were present inside the building. Meanwhile, Billing and I hid behind vehicles that were parked near the train station.

After monitoring the house, the soldier came back to us to tell us that for him there should be no real dangers. I look at the soldier and tell him.

— The Second Lieutenant will not be able to go over the wall. We have to be opened the entrance gate of the house.

— I take care of it. I will knock on the door and ask for help.

— You have to be careful, soldier. You never know.

— Don't worry, I speak French very well and without an accent.

What I didn't know was that this soldier although he was wearing a British army uniform was actually a French soldier who had been repatriated to England from Dunkirk. He hurried through the wall and went to knock on the door of the house. For our safety, Second Lieutenant Billing and I remain hidden. What is striking is that from where I am I can hear the conversation between the woman and the French soldier.

— Good morning, madam, I am sorry to disturb you at such a late hour. I am a free France soldier, and we were parachuted a little earlier. I am accompanied by two other people, and we are looking for refuge. Because there is our head of mission who is injured in the ankle. Can you help us?

— But naturally, do you want to open the gate for whoever is coming in?

— Yes, indeed please.

The woman took the keys and gave them to the soldier who left to open the gate. He beckons us to come. The Second Lieutenant stood up and we advanced towards the gate. Then we entered the courtyard of the property. The young child looks out the window to monitor the area to make sure no Germans were in sight.

The woman asked us to enter the house quickly. She looked at Second Lieutenant Billing and told her.

— You should have put on a civilian outfit.

Billing smiles and answers her.

— Madam, I am a soldier of the king, and a civilian outfit is not comfortable to jump out of a plane.

— I'm going to give you my husband's civilian outfits like that, you won't be as showy. Imagine if you come across a German patrol. With your uniform, you would have been arrested.

I look at this young woman and I think maybe we were the same age. She was very friendly. I notice that she is talking about her husband in the past tense. The young woman looked at me and said.

— For you, I'm going to give you some of my dresses. You have to be about the same size. You are, of French nationality madam?

I give him a smile and answer.

— No, madam, I am British.

The young woman looked at me and smiled.

— I have to tell you... That your expression in French and remarkable. You don't have a pronounced accent. It may be believed that you have always lived in France. This is quite surprising.

— Thank you very much, know that since I was ten years old, I spend my holidays in France in the Bordeaux region. Besides, it was there that we had to go.

— How to tell you? You are relatively far from Bordeaux. Here, it is Meung-sur-Loire in the Loiret department. We are about twenty kilometers from the city of Orleans. Bordeaux is about four hundred kilometers from here.

Second Lieutenant Billing surprised replies.

— What? Four hundred kilometers? Radio operator, get in touch with London and inform them. Remember to ask them the question, how can we reach Bordeaux and its region?

The radio operator put the suitcase on the table. Then he took out of the suitcase various elements. An antenna, a walrus flap and an amplifier and he laid them out on the table.

The young French soldier began sending a Morse code message to London. After a few lines of his message, we heard in the street, vehicles parked. With the window open we realized that they were Germans. Indeed, a voice shouted orders in the language of Goethe. Immediately, the woman told the Radio Operator to cut off communication with London. Which he does immediately. He disconnected all connections. The woman tells us.

— Follow me quickly. I will hide you in the cellar behind a fake wall.

We follow it as best we can. She guides us through a small corridor that leads to a door, which guides us to steps. We went down the steps with the suitcase with the elements of the radio half closed. To tell you, I was the one who had the antenna in my hand. We arrived in front of a wall. We all came to a standstill. The woman arrived and rotated the wall. We entered and there we saw that other people were present. She tells us.

— Entered and especially after you do not move anymore. Again, a small request did not speak. You will be safe.

The woman closed the wall behind us. The people who were with us in this room, stared at us. Among them were children. The Second Lieutenant looks at me and says in a low voice.

— But who are his people and why are they hidden here?" There, I don't know what to think.

Suddenly, a man of a certain age locked up with us began to talk with a young man. I notice that they speak to each other in Hebrew. To be exact in Yiddish. The young French soldier says.

— My Lieutenant, do you understand what they are saying? Because it's not French and I don't understand.

— Sergeant, I will be honest with you. I have no idea what language it is.

— It's Yiddish. It is a language that the Jewish people of Central Europe use. It is strange that he speaks this language.

— Lauren, did you understand what they're saying?

— Yes, in part. He wonders if one is being chased by the Germans and if it is because one is Jewish.

— You can try to explain Lauren to them.

I approached the two men and spoke in a low voice.

— We are British. We are on a mission. Don't be afraid of us. We are against the Germans.

The younger of the two men replied.

— We are Poles. Polish Jews to tell you all. We fled Poland shortly after the Germans arrived. The Germans gathered many Jews from our small town, women, men, and children. They took them to the forest and there... Bang... Bang...

They shot them all. They're all dead. Why at the beginning of the war, did your country let us down?

— Sir, believe me. We apologize for our naivety. But King Neville Chamberlain's Prime Minister made a big mistake as we now know. That is why the King's new Prime Minister is Winston Churchill. Hey Lauren.

— What did he say? Ask Billing.

— They are Polish Jews. The Germans arrested all the Jews in their city and drove them into the forest to kill them.

— But his people whom the Germans killed were soldiers?

— I don't think my Lieutenant. He told me about women, men, and children.

— Children... Germans are repugnant men. Sorry, excuse me, but it disgusts me. Say the French soldier.

— My Lieutenant, do you think London is aware of the actions of the Germans in Poland?

— I don't know, but we have to inform them. I hope that this patrol will leave soon, that its information will be communicated to London.

The Germans have been in the area for forty minutes. He searches all the houses. All of a sudden, we hear the door that leads to the cellar open. Then boot noises sounded above us. It was a German soldier who went down the steps to control the cellar. The thud of a conversation above us, informs us of events.

— So, ma'am, you say that there are only you and your son in the house right now.

— Yes, that is correct, Mr. Officer.

— You haven't seen anyone or heard the DCA shooting a few miles from here.

— You know the shooting... I'm used to it... After all... You shoot us when the population evacuates to safety.

— Madam, it is not on the population that the German army fires... It was on the soldiers hiding among the population that our planes fired.

—Tell the children who saw their parents die as a result of the many air attacks by your fighter jets.

— Madam, you don't like German soldiers, do you?

— I'm not going to lie to you. Exactly. I do not carry in my heart the members of the army who killed my husband.

— This is war, madam, there are inevitably deaths.

— Tell my son.

The boots of the German soldier who had descended into the room can be heard coming up. A snap of the boot heel is heard. The latter says.

— Oberfürer, no one in the rooms except the wife and her son.

We hear again a snap of the heel of the boot and the voice said.

— Madam, goodbye. If you see unknown people in the area called the gendarmerie who will inform us. Heil Hitler.

The sounds of boots are heard less and less loudly. You can hear the engine sound starting and the vehicles moving away. After a few minutes, footsteps can be heard again on the stairs. The wall began to rotate again. It was the young woman who was there. She tells us.

— You can go out now.

We go up the stairs to get to a small room. Second Lieutenant Billing asked.

— Madam, the people who are currently in your hiding place... What do you do with his people? And why are they hiding in your home?

— I hide them! I am a member of a network that aims to protect people of the Jewish faith or people who are being chased by German soldiers and the police.

— Radio, please pass on the information to London for their releases, that what its people have told us.

— In your place, I would wait. The Germans may have left, but from my experience, I know they are never far away.

— Madam, it is that we have a mission. London must be informed about the German troops in the Bordeaux sector.

— Waited five minutes to be sure.

While the young woman says her words. Outside a German radio detection vehicle park, escorted by a sidecar of the German feldgendarmerie. I stood at the window and looked at the vehicles. I waved to Second Lieutenant Billing.

— She is right, there are still German vehicles in the sector.

The young woman approached the window and said.

— See? They never leave, immediately the Germans. In addition if your radio would be in communication. You will have been discovered. Do you have French identity documents?

— Yes, they are there.

— Well, we see right away that they are false! Tampons are no longer like that. In case of control of the French gendarmerie or the Germans, you would be unmasked.

— Sorry, but in London we don't have the models of French identity documents.

— I'll see what I can do. I will come back.

The woman left the house. She crosses the gate and there one of the two feldgendarme comes to meet her.

— Ausweispapier bitte!

She took a document out of her bag and gave it to the German soldier.

— Behold.

The soldier looked at the document. Then he gives it back to the young woman.

— Danke schöne.

Then she leaves. I watch through the window waiting for the young woman to return. Second Lieutenant Billing worried when he wondered where the young woman was gone. I see him pacing in the room where the young woman told us to wait for her return. The German soldiers of the feldgendarmerie continue to carry out their checks of passers-by. Everyone going to the station was checked and had to present a document. I think it is a pass to have the right to travel. After fifteen minutes, the sidecar started in a huge noise. Then the truck and the sidecar left. The young woman arrives five minutes later. She returned to the house. She takes off her vest, gives me a little smile and says.

— It's okay, I managed. You will have your papers tomorrow afternoon. This afternoon, a man will come to collect your identity photos to then put them on tomorrow's one. This way, you will be able to move around our area without fear of the controls of the German troops.

— Thank you for your help, Madam. Besides, what's your name?

— Call me Martine.

— So thank you very much, Martine. But that's your real name Martine?

— It's nothing. Let's say it's an assumed name. Above all, I don't like what Pétain, and the Germans are doing.

A few hours later in a sunny afternoon, a man, who looked like he was in his thirties, showed up at the door and knocked on the door of the house. He reminds me of Second

Lieutenant Billing when he first came to my parents' house. Martine, a young woman, with whom we have taken refuge, leaves to open the door. The man hurried home.

— Martine, hello, it was Pierre who told me to come and see you. He told me it was urgent.

— Thank you, Louis, for coming so quickly. I need a special service please.

— Tell me Martine. What do you want me to do?

— I would like identity papers for 3 people. They are one woman and two men.

— You know it gets more and more risky if I get caught, I would be arrested and questioned by the authorities.

— Please Louis. Do it for me. It is a group of three Englishmen. If they are caught for themselves, it is death for sure.

— Expect the English? You know that currently there is a German detachment in town to look for its English.

The Radio Operator entered the small living room of the house.

— Oh, forgive me.

— Martine, he's one of the Englishmen.

— This offends me, I am as French as you are. Of course, I am in the English uniform, but I am French.

— In addition, their identity documents are very badly done. It would be taken in a very short time either by the gendarmes or by the Germans with such documents.

— On the false papers they currently have with them, they must have photos?

The young woman shows the documents that the English had in their possession.

— Look, they are very badly done.

The man looked at the documents that the young woman had shown him. He looks at Martine and then his gaze returns to the documents.

— Indeed, it is a real disaster his identity documents. If they walk around with that as an identity document on our streets. They will be arrested on the spot. I will take the photographs to make them the most successful. Believe me Martine, it will be easy not to do worse than these documents.

Louis took photographs of the documents that the London services had made for the members of the small commando. And he explains to Martine.

— Martine tomorrow afternoon, I would bring the identity documents back to the clock café. Know that you should send someone in your place. I heard a gendarme speak this morning with one of his colleagues. He finds that you are seen going back and forth in the city without you buying much.

— Of course, Peter. I'm going to send someone to pick them up tomorrow afternoon around fourteen o'clock, will that suit you?

— Fourteen hours is perfect for me. If it's a woman, lend her your blue dress and the yellow vest. This will allow me to recognize the person quickly. If it's a man, give him your father's cane and one of your husband's suits with a black hat.

— I would do as you tell me Louis. Pay attention to yourself.

The man smiles and says.

— But I'm always careful.

Louis comes out of the house and looks into the distance if the streets were safe. Then, he goes down the few steps that separate him from the alley of the courtyard and opens the gate to exit. It heads towards the center of the small town.

86

Project: Light of the Night

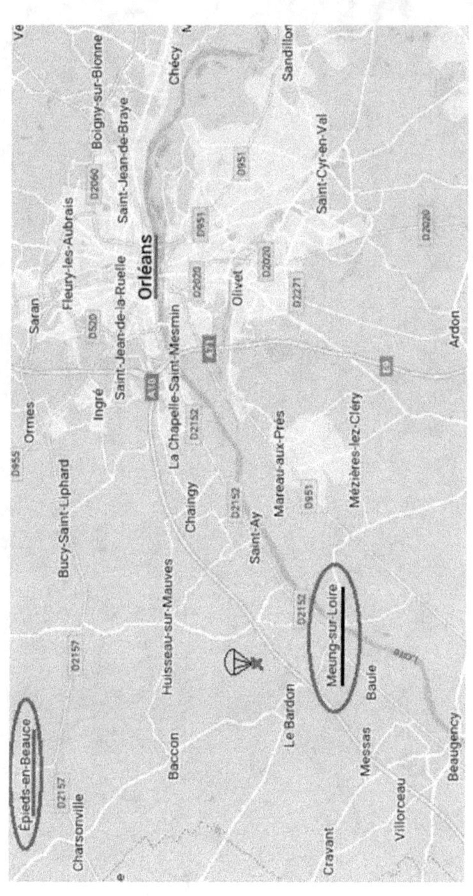

The "x" indicates the site of the commando's parachuting.

4. CHANGES OF PLAN.

We were all in the big dining room. Martine looked at Second Lieutenant Billing and said.

— Sir, I need a service. Like myself, I have done you a service.

— Say, what is it about madame?

— Well, yesterday morning, you know, I went to town to meet someone for the reason that if you go out in case of checking your papers, you will betray.

— Yes, I remember that. In the afternoon, a man came here to get the photographs and criticize the people who make us our false papers.

— Yes, Louis is very picky about the quality of false documents. You have to be sure that he has no resentment against the English. Some time ago, a man to whom he had to make false papers did not want to wait and paid a person for false papers. Unfortunately, the person worked for the Germans. She was arrested and executed. So he's picky.

— I didn't know, I'm sorry.

— Louis, yesterday, told me that French gendarmes were talking about me. That I will be watched! I ask that you send a member of your team to retrieve the false papers.

Second Lieutenant Billing looked at Laurent. Afterwards, he looked at Lauren and then said.

—I don't speak French well enough. Laurent is due to send the messages for London this afternoon. All that's left is you, Lauren.

— All right, I would. I don't know how to get to the meeting place.

— Don't worry, I'll explain, it's very simple. I will lend you one of my dresses and a small vest, I am sure it will delight you.

After the meal, Martine leads Lauren to a room and shows her the outfit she has prepared for him. This is a beautiful blue colored dress with a small white flower print. A pair of small ballerinas of white color and a vest of light-yellow color. She told him.

— I'm going to make you a nice hairstyle. You're going to be beautiful. You will even turn heads as you pass.

I can't remember the last time I took time to take care of myself. I think the last time was a few days before my older brother Isaac left for France. It was my little mom who had my hair that day. It was strange. I don't know how to explain it. I was with his memories both sad and his memories were also pleasant. I was thinking about my big brother and my parents. That I would love to hear their voices so much! See their faces and be able to touch them just for a moment, even, only one minute.

Martine started styling my hair. She was so sweet, like my mother. She placed my hair back and made two small braids on the side. Martine joined the two braids at the back of my skull. She helps me put on the dress that I think is beautiful. Then I put on the vest. The vest was so soft, and it smelled so good. I think this has the smell of lilac in the middle of summer when the wind blows on the small flowers and spreads their sweet scents. Martine smiled at me and said.

— And now one important thing. Well, I don't have much left, but a woman is a woman and perfume are very important.

At his words, I make a smile. I'm sure my eyes were light green, and she smiled. It is true that before the beginning of the war I liked to perfume myself. Martine took a bottle out of the bedside table near her bed. She presses on the pear of the vaporizer. This makes me bathe in a droplet cloud of its fragrance. This perfume had a candy smell. It reminds me of the scent of cotton candy stick. It's such a pleasant smell.

— Your perfume has a nice smell.

— Thank you. In any case, I can tell you that this outfit suits you divinely. On you, it is splendid.

— Thank you very much.

— If you wish, I will give it to you.

— I can't accept it, she's so beautiful.

— I insists. It looks great on you.

— But your husband is not going to be happy if you gave it to me.

Martine lowers her head and says.

— My husband won't tell you anything. He died. When the Germans arrived in Meung-sur-Loire. My husband and several men chased away to bring back food. They found themselves, facing the German advance and like all French. My husband did not accept the presence of the Germans and with his friends they shot and killed Germans. In retaliation, the Germans after capturing them executed them on the banks of the Loire.

— Sorry, I'm sorry.

— It doesn't matter, you couldn't know. That's why I hate Germans. Also because I know how much they do to people who do not fit into their visions of the ideal world according to them. You know, Lauren, a friend gave me the book that

Chancellor Adolf Hitler wrote when he was in prison. The book is called Mein Kampf. It's horrible what he plans to do.

— I haven't read it and you know, I'm against the Germans for several reasons. My older brother Isaac is missing. The Germans bombed my city and my parents died.

— Isaac... Is it a Hebrew name?

— Yes... I am Jewish.

— Do you know that the Germans want to get rid of all the Jews in Europe?" When I say rid of, it is not to say the word killed. The people I hide come from Poland and there the Germans kill all people of the Jewish faith.

— We are aware of that. That is why I am the one who is going to the appointment just now. The radio station must inform London of its information.

— Promise me that you will be careful.

— I promise you.

— Now I'm going to explain how to get to the meeting place. It will be in a café. Leaving the house, you will leave on the right. You will then arrive on a highway. You cross this road, and you continue in a small alley. It takes you to a large square. The square is slightly sloping. You go up this slope and you will see a street that passes under a large clock. You walk down this street to a café which will be on your left. Then you will need to order a coffee. If you ask for tea, people will know that you are not French and nowadays you have to be wary of people. A man will come and give you the identity papers. Afterwards, you come back here. Did you understand how to do it?

— I understood the plan perfectly. I'm going to go.

— I says.

— Excuse me?

— It's a French expression that means good luck.

— A little weird as an expression. In our country, this would be considered an insult.

— I would not have allowed myself to insult you.

Lauren takes a deep breath. She opens the door of the house and goes down the few steps of the steps of the house. She opens the gate of the courtyard and goes out into the street. Lauren was happy to see the sunlight of March. The temperature was pleasant for a month of March. She leaves in the direction that Martine had indicated to her. The young woman was cheerful and every time she met a person, she said hello to them. She walks with a smile on her face. She arrived at the place where a large clock must be. Lauren looked over the passage of the road. Then she said.

— It's in that direction!

After a few minutes of walking, I enter the café that Martine told me. I see a table without anyone. I sit on the chair that faces the front door of the café. The waiter comes to meet me and tells me.

— Madam, good morning... What do you want to drink?

— I'll have a coffee please.

The waiter left to prepare my drink. After a few minutes of waiting, the waiter comes back with my cup of coffee. I start drinking my coffee. When all of a sudden, French gendarmes and men dressed in raincoats enter the café. One of the men said in a firm and strong voice.

— This is an identity check. Please all take out your identity documents!

Worry is starting to win me over. How will I do without his documents? I risk being arrested and handed over to the Germans. The gendarme walks to the table next to mine. At the table, there was a man and a young woman. The gendarme looks at them and says.

– Didn't you hear? Your papers!

The man looks at the gendarme and gives him his identification documents. The gendarme looks at them and stares at the man and the woman. And he tells them.

— You are Jews! What do you do in this café? Coffees are forbidden to youpins!

The gendarme looks at his colleague and tells him.

— Look at those two! The Youpins believe they are at home in France. We embark them to make them pass the desire to start again.

Two gendarmes approach the young couple and take them by the arm. The young woman struggles while trying to stay in the chair. So let the man gesticulate in all directions. One of the gendarmes took out his baton and hit the woman and the man violently. And then they took the two inanimate bodies out of the café. The gendarme who had ordered the arrest of this young couple turned to the owner of the café and told him.

— So you serve the youpins?

— How do I know if they are Jewish?

— Yes... Yes... You risk the closure of your café if you serve the youpins! You know that!

— Yes gendarme.

Then the gendarme turns to me and looks at me and says.

— Tell me you... I've never seen you in the area. Your identity papers!

I'm starting to get scared because I don't have the fake ID documents on me. The gendarme looks at me and says in a louder voice.

— Are you deaf? I asked you for your papers! Otherwise I take you for a little interrogation! You're Jewish, is that right?

I feel my heart beating harder and harder. I didn't know what to do and I'm starting to tremble. A man in a light raincoat enters the café. And he approaches my table, and he says.

— Gendarme, do you have a problem with my wife?

I look at the man and I tell myself that I had never seen her and yet the man tells the gendarme that I am his wife. The gendarme looks at the man and tells him.

— Is it your wife? I've never seen her here. And you, you have your identity papers? Are you a youpin?

— Yes, I have my papers, Mr. Gendarme. And know that I do not like to be called youpin. Hold on, here are my identity documents!

The man pulled out of the inside of his raincoat a card. The gendarme took the documents abruptly. The man smiled and stared at the gendarme and said to him. The gendarme opened his eyes wide and then lowered his head.

— Gendarme you have nothing to say to me? You still called me "youpin" in front of my wife. In addition, know that the commander of your gendarmerie and a childhood friend. And that my wife and I have to have dinner with him tonight. And know that I always have my wife's identity documents with me. That is why she cannot give them to you at your request.

— I am sorry, Mr. Inspector. I didn't know. But she didn't inform me that she was your wife and that you had her identity documents.

— My wife has learned not to respond to rude people. Were you badly raised with her, Mr. Gendarme? You know she will tell me if it is, and I could not leave it without talking to your superior. You understand?

— I assure you, Mr. Inspector, I was polite to her!

— Is it true, this gendarme lies?

— Yes, I swear to you!

The man posing as my husband looks at me, gives me a smile and a wink. I have the impression that I am bothering the gendarme.

— Juliette, my dear, tell me this gendarme was polite to you?

— He said I was a youpine!

— What? Gendarme you had the audacity to tell my wife that she was a youpine? How dare you say this about the wife of a police inspector? You want me to summon you to my offices in Orleans. And that I personally take care of your case. Say the man screaming.

Then he turns to the other gendarmes and tells them.

— Know that I don't like it at all! And that I will summon you all to Orleans and I will all one by one you question then I would summon the members of your families and your friends to question them. Believe me it will not be a pleasure for you, but also for them. Do you know the methods we use? Otherwise I could let you know them by testing them on you and your families.

— We apologize inspector. Please be indulgent.

— You ask me to be indulgent when you claim that my wife, my sweet and tender wife is a Jew?" No way!

— Please inspector. Say the gendarme in tears knowing that the interrogations of the Orléans police were harsh and very violent.

— You didn't even apologize to my lovely wife.

— Sorry, madam, for naming you from youpin.

— That's not enough for me! You will get on your knees, apologize to my wife, and then kiss her feet!

— I beg you inspector.

— Either it is, or you will be tomorrow morning in my office at six o'clock.

The gendarme knelt down in front of Lauren. Lauren gave a slight smile. The gendarme in front of everyone present starts kissing Lauren's feet. And while keeping his head down he tells her.

— Madam, I apologize for insulting you as a Jew.

The inspector grabbed the gendarme and picked him up brutally and pushed him out of the café and told him.

— Now cleared from here before I get upset and go back on my decision.

The gendarmes made a military salute and left. The man comes back to the table where I was sitting and says to me.

— I'm sorry for what his morons told you. He turns to the waiter and tells him.

— I want a coffee please.

— Yes, all of them right away, inspector!

While the waiter prepares the coffee. The man said to me.

— Take under the table.

The man handed me documents under the table. I take them. The waiter then arrives with the coffee. The man drank the coffee and said to me.

— My dear, I'm sorry, but I'm going to have to go see the commander of the gendarmerie brigade. Go to your cousin Martine's house and wait for me there please. I have important things to do with my childhood friend who heads the gendarmerie.

— Well, I'm going to my cousin's house and I'm waiting for you.

I get up and head to Martine's house. During the journey, I thought of the young couple who were arrested by the gendarmes. What will happen to them? But I also think of this man I didn't know and who saved me from the gendarmes. It could have been dangerous for him. But I found it so amusing that on my way home I can't help but smile as I remember the gendarme who was on his knees in front of me and kissed my feet and apologized for calling me Jewish.

When I arrived at Martine's house, I went back. Martine was waiting for me and worried that I wouldn't arrive as quickly as she thought.

—What happened? Martine asks.

— There was a control on the part of the gendarmerie. That's fine, the man who joined me with the false papers saved me. He even told a gendarme to get on his knees and kiss my feet, asking forgiveness for saying I was Jewish.

— What? Say Second Lieutenant Nigel Billing.

— I bet you he took out his police card. It must be said that Cédric has a lot of humor. Martine explains.

— How do you know he pulled out a police card?" Hey Lauren.

— For a gendarme to get on his knees and kiss your feet and ask for your forgiveness, it is only a policeman who can do it. A resident could not do it without the gendarmes bothering him.

— In any case, it was funny. Hey Lauren.

Laurent, the radio operator enters the room where the small group is. He looks at Second Lieutenant Nigel and tells him.

— My Lieutenant, I have just finished the transmission with the London Headquarters. Following the information we have given them; London informs us that we are changing our plan. We no longer have to go to Bordeaux. We have to stay here to collect information about this sector.

— All right, but, London, told you what information we need to collect? Or what should we do with this group of Poles?

— London has only said that they will contact us within twelve hours to provide us with further information on the continuation of our mission.

— They are aware that we are on a territory occupied by the Germans and that we are wanted? Second Lieutenant Billing asks.

— I'm sorry my Lieutenant, but that's all they said.

— You can stay here as long as you please. Rest assured you are safe here.

— Thank you very much, madam! Say Lieutenant Billing.

— I told you to call me Martine.

— So, thank you very much, Martine.

The team moved into Martine's house now that the London Headquarters had instructed them not to try to reach the Bordeaux city area. Hearing this news, Lauren was a little sad. She had hoped to see her friend Marie Duval again when she could arrive in the Bordeaux region. Because it has now been nine months since she heard from her friend Marie. In the head of the young woman constantly wonders what becomes of her friend Marie. Did the latter stay in Bordeaux following the arrival of German troops? Where was it moved during the advance of the Germanic troops? Has she managed to realize her dream of becoming a singer? Did Mary tell Robert that she loved him?

This anthology of questions turned in loop in the head of the young woman. How to let her friend Marie Duval know that she was there? Certainly several hundred kilometers from his friend Marie. But she was there, in France. She would love to see her friend Marie Duval again. He was the last person in her past she wanted to see. She wondered if a letter posted from the France itself would reach her friend Marie Duval. And so she decided to ask Martine the question.

— Martine?

— Yes Lauren?

— May I ask you a question?

— But of course Lauren.

— I have a friend in France. She lives in the city of Bordeaux. I wanted to see her again during our mission in the Bordeaux region. Do you know if the mail between here and Bordeaux works?

— Yes, the mail between Meung-sur-Loire and Bordeaux works. It is true that mail takes much longer to be delivered during this period. But it is also because there is the control service that opens the letters and looks in the writings if people would not have information about British soldiers hiding on French territory.

— There are other British soldiers besides us France? Stunned ask the young woman.

— Of course, Lauren, you are not the first British troops I see in our area. Other British soldiers are hidden a little further away in a small town in the canton. They managed to bypass the Germans during the encirclement of the city of Dunkirk.

— You mean that British soldiers have fled Dunkirk and are not hiding far from here?

— Well yes! That is what I am telling you. But why didn't you tell us?

— I didn't know you'd be interested in knowing.

Young Lauren starts thinking even more. Martine had just told him that several British soldiers were in the area. And, that its soldiers were located in Dunkirk at the time that the German soldiers had surrounded the British troops on the beaches at the time of the evacuation organized by the army of His Majesty King George VI. The young woman can't help but think of her older brother Isaac. Isaac was in Dunkirk; he had not been able to board because the boat that led him to the repatriation ship with sinking following an attack by a fighter plane of the German army. But his body had never been found. It was on the statement of a soldier of his unit that Lauren's brother had been reported missing. So no one knew if he was actually dead, wounded or captured by the troops of the German army.

— Lieutenant Billing must be informed! We must be informed that we have British troops close to our position.

— Yes, now that you tell me I think it would perhaps be an asset for all of us.

The two young women head into the radio operator's room. Second Lieutenant Nigel Billing was with the operator to try to see if they get more information about their potential mission. Lauren looks at Second Lieutenant Billing and tells him.

— Lieutenant, I have important information for London, and this is very urgent!

— What's going on Lauren?" Say Lieutenant.

— There are British soldiers near here! Lauren explains.

— How are there British Crown soldiers near here. Reply the Lieutenant.

— Yes, they are about twenty or twenty-five kilometers from here. In a farm in the town of Epieds-en-Beauce. Martine explains.

— Laurent! Contact London about the emergency message frequency and tell them this information.

— Well my Lieutenant I transmit the message to them.

The radio operator, Laurent, began to transmit the information to London.

— Now we need to know how to get in touch with his British soldiers. And above all to do it without being noticed.

A short moment of silence was heard. Then suddenly Martine said.

— There's Cedric! With his function as a police inspector, he can go to all places in the Loiret department.

— And how will this help us?" Second Lieutenant Billing asks.

— Lauren knows him! She just has to make it look like it's his wife and go with him to the farm. And there she will meet the British soldiers. What do you think, Lieutenant Billing?

— Yes, that seems to me to be a possibility. Say Billing.

— We can talk about it tonight with Cédric. That way, he will tell us if this idea is feasible without too much danger.

— How will we talk about this idea with Cédric. Lauren asks.

— Lauren, it was you who told me Cédric will pick you up to go to dinner with his childhood friend the Commander of the gendarmerie.

— Yes, but, I think, who said that to make our story more realistic.

—That is to say, logically it had to be me who had to go to this dinner. But it is better that it is you who go to dinner in case you meet one of the gendarmes of just now.

— Well, I understand. Hey Lauren.

— Don't worry Lauren. The Commander of the Gendarmerie is on our side. It is thanks to them that you have true-false identity papers. I tell you true-false by what you have real identity documents, but with false information. No German or policeman or gendarme will be able to tell the difference.

    — Okay, then I'll go with him. Hey Lauren.

Control of the Feldgendarmerie.

5. CHILDREN AND SOLDIERS ARE HIDDEN.

In the early evening, the man Lauren had met rather during the day arrives at Martine's house. Lauren had enjoyed the young man during the short time she had spent with him in the café. The man entered Martine's house. The young woman brings Cédric into the living room of the house. Lauren had kept her beautiful outfit that she wore that morning. The young man says.

— You are still as magnificent as this morning, mademoiselle.

— Thank you very much.

— I am sorry for what happened this morning at the café. I'm also sorry I didn't show up. My name is Cédric.

— Me, it's Lauren. I am delighted to meet you, Cédric.

— No, your name is Juliettete! I remind you of that. Be careful! It can be dangerous not to use the name you have on your identity documents!

— Excuse me! I thought you'd like to know my real name.

— Know that I know your first name, I am the one who makes your identity papers.

— I didn't know, sorry.

Martine looks at Lauren, then she notices that the young woman is blushing. Immediately, she told him.

— Lauren is a woman who is very beautiful isn't it, Cedric! Can't you think?

— That's right, you're right, Martine. I would not say the opposite.

At her words, Lauren blushed even more. Seeing this, Martine starts laughing. And said to Lauren.

— Lauren, don't you think your husband is handsome?

— My husband, I'm not married, Martine!

— I'm talking about Cedric! Technically for the gendarmes you are married.

— Oh yes, it's true I had forgotten, sorry.

— Lauren is careful I remind you that tonight you are going to the gendarmerie brigade with Cédric. You must do everything to make this story as real as possible it will prevent the gendarmes from discovering that it is false.

— I'll be careful.

— Rest assured, the Brigade Commander is a childhood friend. And he's with us, I mean he's in our resistance network. Although, he like me, risk a lot. Up to the death penalty for that.

In her words Lauren looked at the man and understood that this young man and the members of his network risked their lives consciously to save the lives of no one like Lauren,

Laurent, Second Lieutenant Billing, and the Jewish people hidden in Martine's basement. She finds it an act of courage to put their lives on the line to rescue people they don't know. Martine looks at Cedric and tells him.

— Cedric...

— Yes Martine?...

— I talked to Lauren and the other members of her group about the British Soldiers we hide on the farm in Epieds-en-Beauce. His senior officer, Lieutenant Billing, wants Lauren to go to meet them. Can you arrange this please?

— I have no objection, but I will have to accompany her to prevent her from being caught.

— How many British soldiers did he have?

— There are six British soldiers. But only one of them speaks French. All of them managed to get out of the hell of Dunkirk.

But London was not informed that British soldiers were hidden by French resistance fighters. Hey Lauren.

— Sorry, but you have to understand us, Lauren. They were regularly changed hiding places to prevent them from being captured by the Germans. We are looking for a solution to send them back to England.

—I understands.

— It's soon time, are you ready, Mrs. Juliettete Delfleur?

— Who?

— Lauren is you, Juliettete Delfleur! Say Martine laughing.

Lauren began to blush again as Cedric presented her elbow to place her hands on.

—We have to go to the Commander of the gendarmerie brigade. Remember to remember your first and last name. Because we go through the guard of the gendarmerie and then see my friend. And they will definitely ask you for your identity documents.

The young woman goes out accompanied by her false husband Cédric. And together, they head to the gendarmerie brigade. In front of the gendarmerie barracks, Lauren makes a stop. It was as if she was paralyzed. The fear of crossing the gendarmes blocks Lauren for long minutes. Suddenly, Cedric tells Lauren.

— Something scares you?

— I am not reassured to return to this place.

—Don't worry. You are with me.

The duo enters the gendarmerie brigade and presents themselves to the guard. Cédric takes out of his raincoat his police inspector card and tells the soldier of the reception.

— Please inform your brigade commander that I have arrived.

The young soldier takes note of his name and goes to see the commander of the brigade. Cédric's childhood friend comes out of his office and heads to the brigade's reception.

— My friend Cedric! you finally agree to visit me at my modest little gendarmerie brigade.

— It's better late than never Alain.

— Yes, you're right. Juliette... You accompany your husband, I'm delighted! Can I tell you that you are more and more beautiful? Cedric, I compliment your wife I hope you won't blame me?

— No, rest assured Alain! I know Juliette is beautiful so it's normal for other men to find her splendid.

On the words spoken by Cédric, the young woman begins to blush. Seeing Lauren blush, Cedric can't help but say.

— Every time she is complimented, she can't help but smile. Although we have been married for six years. I find that too cute.

—Yes, that's right. But Juliette you know that you are beautiful. Cedric is lucky to have married you.

— Yes, thank you very much for his compliments. Note, I think it is also beautiful. Say, the young woman looking at Cedric.

Cedric surprised by Lauren's words begins to blush. This reaction of the man makes his childhood friend start laughing.

— Cedric, it's not just your wife who blushes too.

Alain starts laughing out loud. The gendarmes present at the reception watch their superiors laugh. His last had never seen their officer laugh or even joke with a person. Alain was considered a rather cold person and did not have a great attraction for humor. Alain opened the small door that separates the reception desk with the area of people coming to the brigade. Lauren and Cédric enter the common area of the gendarmes.

At the same time, the gendarme who rather in the day had carried out the control in the café arrived. The latter saw the young woman and Cédric. He passes by their side, lowering his head thinking that he would not be recognized. But it was without counting on Cédric who called him.

— Gendarme! As we meet again. I told you that I would come to your brigade tonight.

— What's going on, Cedric? The officer asks.

— It is your gendarme here who tells my princess Juliette that she is a Jew!

— What?

The Commander turns to the gendarme and tells him.

— Is it true what my childhood friend and police inspector from Orléans, Constable Belville, just said?

— My Lieutenant, I apologized afterwards.

— But you know who you're dealing with before you tell people they're Jews.

— We carry out an identity check. And she didn't have her identity documents with her.

— And this allows you to tell the wife of a police inspector that his wife is a Jew?

— No, my Lieutenant.

— Do not punish this gendarme Alain too much, it is true that I leave my identity papers to Cédric because I do not take my purse with me. And he only did his job. He couldn't know.

— Constable Belville, you can thank the inspector's wife and my childhood friend Cédric. Juliette, please accept my apologies.

— It's nothing, I assure you Alain.

— Constable Belville, during the coming month you will be on a guard every day and you will receive only half a salary for daring to say that the wife of a police inspector is a Jew.

— At your command, my Lieutenant.

— Let's go to dinner now friends.

The trio takes the direction of the Commander's house which is located in the backyard of the gendarmerie brigade. All three enter the house. The Lieutenant's wife had prepared the table as if it were a feast day. The Commander's wife knows Cedric and had that Lauren was not his wife because Cedric was not married. All took their seats around the table. Lauren offers the Lieutenant's wife to help her with the service. The woman tells Lauren.

— Please sit at the table. I will take care of the service. Don't worry, ma'am.

— Cedric, you know that the Germans are looking for the group of Englishmen who have jumped on the sector. They ask us to find them and deliver them.

— Lauren is one of the British soldiers.

— I suspect Cédric, but she has to be careful. It's like your cousin Martine. People say that she is a resistance fighter and against Marshal Pétain.

— You know his opinion on Pétain Alain.

— I fully understand Martine and I agree with her. Pétain is a treaty vis-à-vis the French people! Say Alain's wife.

— Tomorrow we would have to go to the farm of Epieds-en-Beauce to see the English. Say Cedric.

— Cédric, I can't come with you tomorrow to Epieds-en-Beauce, sorry. There is the commander of the feldgendarmerie who comes to pay us a little visit. If I could take a grenade and blow it up next to him.

— No Alain it would be too dangerous for you and your wife. But there are also the people around and without counting on the reprisals that the Germans would inflict on the population.

— Yes, but you understand Cedric! I'm tired of seeing his rats walking around like they were at home.

— I understand you Alain's. But we must think that we are not alone. We will make them leave France one day. I promise!

Young Lauren listened to the conversation without saying a word. The wife of the Commander of the gendarmerie looks at her and tells her.

— I'm sorry for the words we use. I know that may sound nasty to you. But don't you find the presence of his Germans on French soil too harsh?

— Yes, I am aware that the Germans are murderers. I have lost several people in my family to their faults.

— Have you lost family members? Asks the wife of the Commander of the gendarmerie.

— Yes, my brother was a soldier, and he was in Dunkirk. But he did not return to England. And at the beginning of September there was the bombing in north London and my parents' house was destroyed and we with locals pulled my parents' lifeless bodies out of the rubble.

— It's horrible! I hope that one day the Germans will pay for his crimes. Hey, Alain.

— I agree with you, my friend.

The young woman lowered her head and tears could be seen on her cheeks. The Commander's wife took an embroidered handkerchief and gave it to Lauren.

— Hold on my dear. I know it won't bring back the people you lost, but we must not show that the Germans won that would make them far so happy.

— Thank you very much.

— Tomorrow, they have to go to your cousin's farm. Lauren must see the British soldiers. Can you accompany them my dear.

— This will be an honor for me. Do you want to leave around what time?

— The sooner the better. What do you say Lauren? Cedric asks.

— It's the way you want it. I don't know where that is. So I'll let you decide if you want to.

— We leave around 8:30 a.m.? Ask Cédric.

— That suits me perfectly. Say the Commander's wife.

— Me too. Hey Lauren.

— You're going to stay here to sleep like that we'll leave on time. You have to eat now. Tomorrow will be a great day. I am sure of that.

The meal was a treat for Lauren. She had moments of laughter when Cedric explained to Alain and his wife the moment of coffee. And Alain explained to his wife his great theatrical moment that he made at the moment when Constable Belville returned to the gendarmerie brigade. That evening Lauren went to bed for a good hour. And think about your next day. The young woman has a lot of questions. From which region of Britain did the soldiers that the resistance hides come from? Will her soldiers understand that she is on their side? Does one of the soldiers know his brother?

Eight and a half hours is time to set off for Lauren, the Commander's wife, and Cedric. Cédric took the road towards Epieds-en-Beauce. Lauren looked at the scenery with a small smile. She turned to the Commander's wife and told her.

— The France is such a beautiful country. When I was little, I often came with my parents and my older brother. But we were going to Bordeaux.

— Yes, it is true the France to beautiful landscapes, but today this scenery is polluted by the presence of the Germans.

— We're soon here! said Cedric.

Five minutes after he spoke his words. The traction entered a dirt and gravel road. Cedric stopped the car in the center of the farmyard. A tall man who seems a little grumpy came out of the house.

— Lucile! How are you?

In his words the man literally lifted the wife of the Commander of the gendarmerie from the ground and began to kiss her on the cheeks.

Lauren widens her eyes and says to Cedric in a low voice.

— Who is this man? Look, she doesn't even touch the ground with her feet anymore.

— Don't worry, it's his cousin! Say Cedric, bursting out laughing.

— What's going on? Ask the man.

— Antoine, I'm fine thank you, but you scare my friend Juliettete.

— What? Who is Juliettete?

— That's me. Say Lauren in a frail voice.

— Sorry, Mrs. Juliettete. Know that I didn't want to scare you.

— It doesn't matter sir. But can you call me Juliettete?

— If you call me Antoine! I don't like to be told Sir.

— Okay Antoine!

Antoine smiled wide and said.

— There, it's better Juliettete!

The Commander's wife leans towards her cousin Antoine and says to him in a low voice.

— Juliettete is British. She would like to see who you know.

— Oh okay! Please follow me.

The man leads the group to a barn. He takes a fork and moves bales of straw. Below the straw bales, find a hatch. The man taps five times and then he waits, he retypes twice and waits again and then he taps three times with his foot. The man opens the hatch and goes down the steps. He lights two torches and tells us.

— The purpose of the maneuver is for you to follow me. So please come down.

We go down all the steps. The man tells us follow me and beware it is a labyrinth. We walk by the light of two flaming torches. In a maze of corridors. But at each intersection there were three possible paths. Fortunately, Antoine knows the way. We arrived at a door. Again Antoine hit the code. Then he opened the door. It was impressive it made like an alcove. And there are like several pieces connected to each other. Antoine says.

— Hello friends it's me and visitors. A woman from a British commando would like to see you.

The few British soldiers present widened their eyes at Antoine's words. Lauren stepped forward and repeated Antony's words in the language of Shakespeare. The British soldiers began to smile and shake hands. Lauren looked at them and said.

— I am Lauren, I am in the services of King George VI. Together with the other two members of my group, we were shot dead by the German DCA.

— Oh well, you can't drive us back to England. Say a young corporal.

— Unfortunately not for the moment we have to inform London of your presence and then prepare your evacuation.

A man arrives from a nearby room. Lauren feels his presence and from the corner of her right eye and those turning her head slightly to the side. A man says.

— Excuse me, you say how did you name yourself?"

Lauren turns to the man is started to say.

— Lau...

The young woman sees a face. But this cannot be possible. This person cannot be in this hiding place of resistance. Lauren literally faints. After a few moments, Lauren returns to her. Cedric worried asks.

— Lauren are you okay?

— But yes, she's fine. Rest assured; she often does this to make herself interesting. In any case, she does it to us before I leave the house. Say man.

— Who are you please? Ask Cédric.

— Lauren, don't you introduce me to your friends?" My name is Isaac. I am the big brother of the little Princess with sleeping woods.

—Isaac! Is that you?

— No, it's Rabbi Rossemgblum!

— But you had disappeared in Dunkirk! And Mom and Dad, honey, thought you were dead.

— Well, that's nice. I do everything to stay alive to return to England. How are Lauren's parents?

— Sorry Mom and Dad died during the bombing of North London. Say Lauren in a sad voice.

— The Germans will pay for it. Say Isaac.

Lucile, Cedric, and Antoine look at Lauren and Isaac. Cedric says.

— It's great your reunion, but there are also children here who are hidden because they are Jews and if the Germans catch them, they will end up being put on trains that go east. And according to what the information we have been given is not cakes waiting for them, but death!

— You're right Cedric. We must get them all out of France as soon as possible. Hey Lucile.

Isaac leans over to Lauren and says in a low voice.

— This one named Cédric is your boyfriend?

Lauren blushed and replied.

— No, it's the man who pretends to be my husband and he saved my life during a gendarme check in a café a few kilometers from here.

Isaac looks at Cedric and tells him.

— Be careful, this is my little sister. The one and only family I have left. If you hurt him, I kill you.

—Isaac!!

— I reassure you I would never hurt Lauren. Believe me. Cedric answers.

Isaac makes a small smile. Then he looks at his younger sister and tells her.

— Just kidding Lauren.

— How did you leave Dunkirk?

— It's thanks to Simon. His parents died and when our group looked for a hiding place, he provided us with clothes from his late father. Then with him we set out trying to avoid the big cities of France to avoid the German patrols. And we got here.

Antoine fixes them and says.

— You know that not everyone speaks English?

— Forgive us Anthony. But you will understand that I have all just found my brother whom I thought was dead during the Battle of Dunkirk.

— Oh okay and well, finally, one good thing about this terrible war. Say Antoine.

— How so Antoine? Lauren asks.

— I know it can be misinterpreted but I mean it's a beautiful thing for a sister to find her brother she thought was dead. While he was alive and by fate, she finds herself parachuting a few kilometers from the place where her brother is hiding. Antoine explains.

— Sorry I didn't understand what you meant.

Cedric observes the place and says.

— Tell me Antoine... How many people are gathered in this hideout?

— There are six British soldiers, two Belgian soldiers and fifteen children.

— The British and Belgian soldiers I think I can organize an evacuation to Great Britain. But for children it may be harder. Hey Lauren.

— Lauren it's out of the question to leave the children behind. Know that without their help we would be more alive. They formed in small groups. And his party as a scout to collect information about the most secure roads for us. Say Isaac.

— I have to inform the Second Lieutenant to find out how we can do it. It doesn't depend on me or him. London will make the decision. I can't guarantee you anything Isaac.

— If the children stay. We will also stay. Two of them died so that we were alive.

— Cédric we would have to go back to Martine's house quickly so that we know what we can do. But you say that the children collected information?

— Yes, that's what I'm telling you. You know that Germans are not suspicious of young children? They noted the names of the German troops we have come across so far.

— And you think they could do it in the sector?

— Surely!

Cedric and Lauren watch the children gathered in the room where Lauren's older brother came from. Lauren looked at Cedric and said to him.

— Do you think children could help us collect the information London needs? As Isaac says, people will never be suspicious of young children.

— That might be too risky for them.

One of the children overheard the conversation and retorted.

—At least we children can approach the boches without anyone who worries. And we are smarter than adults.

— Maybe, but if you are arrested you will be tortured. And I don't want that. It's too hard for me to assume it. Cedric answers.

— And if it's our own choice! You are not my father so you cannot give me an order!

— It's true I'm not your father. But it is far too dangerous for a child to be part of the resistance.

— Blah... Blah... Blah... Do you still have other nonsense to say? Know that we have managed to survive so far. So, believe me, I know my friends and I are smarter than you.

— You can ask London for advice. And we'll see what they tell us. Hey Lauren.

— Okay.

The young boy smiles wide as he stares at Lauren. The young woman answers him with a smile and asks.

— What is your name?

— Simon! It was I who found the English and Belgian soldiers who were lost.

— Congratulations Simon! My name is Lauren, but here is Juliettete my first name.

— Did you know that there is no relationship between the first name Lauren and the first name Juliettete? In any case, I don't see the relationship.

— Juliettete is the first name I was given here.

— It suits you well. Simon replies.

— We will have to go back to London. But we will come back soon. Hey Lauren.

— You know you're very pretty Juliette. Say Simon.

— Thank you very much, it is a pleasure to hear it. Lauren replies blushingly.

Lucile, Lauren, Cédric, and Antoine leave for the exit of the tunnel that leads to the hideout of the resistance. They come out of the tunnel. Antoine takes the fork and puts the straw bales back above the hatch. Then the small group heads out of the barn. Lucile, the wife of the Commander of the gendarmerie said.

— How are we going to evacuate so many people? This is going to be very difficult and risky.

— Here they are safe. At least for now. Because I saw German trucks going to our neighbor's house. I wonder if he is not a collaborator. Say worried Antoine.

— You have to be careful. Lauren, you keep London informed about your idea. Although I am not too much for the use of children. Otherwise it would be nice to add an adult with one or two children. Cédric explains.

— I will ask London for his opinion. But first I have to talk to the Second Lieutenant to get his opinion on my idea.

—We have to leave. Antoine thank you again for your welcome. Say Cedric shaking hands with Antoine.

— But from nothing it's normal Cedric. Antoine replied.

— Antoine, you will kiss Nadine and the children for me. And tell them that Tata Lucile loves them very much.

— I promises.

Antoine kisses Lucile on her cheeks to say goodbye.

— Antoine, I am delighted to have been able to meet you. And I hope to see you again very soon. Lauren wants to shake his hand.

— In France, Juliettete to say hello or say goodbye a woman and a man kiss on the cheeks. He doesn't shake hands. Antoine explains.

And on his words, he lifts Lauren off the ground and kisses her cheeks. Lucile and Cedric start laughing out loud. Seeing Lauren no longer touch the ground as a little earlier this was the case of Lucile. After kissing Lauren, Antoine rests her on the floor.

— See you very soon, I hope.

The trio took their seats in the car and took the road towards Meung-sur-Loire. Lauren was in a hurry to explain to Second Lieutenant Billing what had happened and her idea. Lauren was like on a little cloud to have found her big brother whom she thought was dead.

British soldiers in Brook (Kent) camp England training area.

6. A PROBLEM.

The small group arrives in Meung-sur-Loire. Lauren hurries out of the car to enter Martine's house. She went so fast that the young woman let her shoe out of her right foot. When Martine and Second Lieutenant Billing saw the young woman rush into the house as quickly as he thought the German soldiers were in pursuit. Martine says.

— What's going on? Are the Germans chasing you?

— No, but we need to send an urgent message to London. And I saw my big brother Isaac again in the hideout of Epieds-en-Beauce.

— But your brother was dead, you told me. Say Martine.

— This is what I thought by the fact that there was no news of him since the Battle of

Dunkirk. Yet he was there.

Cédric and Lucile return to Martine's house. Cedric had taken the time to pick up Lauren's shoe. They enter the small living room where Lauren, Second Lieutenant Billing and radio operator Laurent are.

— Well, she's excited! Hey Lucile.

— Yes, this is surely due to the fact that she found her big brother. Say Cedric.

— So that's true? His older brother is alive and in our hiding place in Epieds-en-Beauce? Martine asks.

— Yes, that is absolutely true. It is the English soldier who does the translations for us. Cédric explains.

— I'm happy for her. Say Martine.

Lauren writes a text on paper and gives it to Second Lieutenant Billing. The latter, takes it and reads it and looks at the young woman. Then he told her.

—Do you really want to convey this message?

— Yes, my Lieutenant!

— Do you want to convey this message?

— What do you not understand in the sentence yes, my Lieutenant?

— Do you want us to say in London that we have six British soldiers, two Belgian soldiers and fifteen children, not to mention the people hiding in the house, or we find ourselves planning an evacuation at the same time as our own evacuation after the collection of information by the children of the Epieds-en-Beauce hideout who will themselves team up with people from the resistance network in the sector?

— That's exactly my Lieutenant!

— But you're crazy! They will never accept!

— May I ask you a question my Lieutenant? Hey Lauren.

— If I tell you no, will it stop you from wanting to ask me your question?"

— Certainly not!

— So, ask your question Lauren.

—Are you suspicious of children walking down the street?

— Of course not!

— Well, do you think the Germans are suspicious of young and frail children who pass by them?

— I don't think so. Children are not fighters, so I don't see why to be suspicious of them.

— So you got my idea.

— I think yes Lauren, I understand your idea. But what do the French think, and will the children agree?

— Lieutenant, know that we French

agree. And as far as the children are concerned, it is they who want us, you help. Hey Lucile.

— I actually see you decided before you even informed me.

— Of course not, I have just informed you.

— I agree if London agrees. Laurent, all you have to do is send this request.

— At your command my Lieutenant!

Laurent took the text of the message and transmitted it as quickly as possible to London. After finishing conveying the message by explaining Lauren's idea, Laurent turns to the Second Lieutenant and says.

— Now we have to wait for London's decision. It won't arrive until tomorrow, I think.

The small group begins to wait for news from London. Night passes and no news from the War Office in London. In the morning, Lucile, the wife of the Commander of the gendarmerie arrives at Martine's house. She enters the house and asks Lauren.

— Lauren, have you seen Martine?

— She is in the small living room with Second Lieutenant Billing.

— Thank you very much Lauren.

— Something is wrong Lucile?

— It's the Germans, they arrested a member of the network. It is located at the FeldKommandantur.

— It's annoying. Do you think he might talk about the members of the network? Lauren asks.

— I don't know. But my husband says that the Germans summoned the Prefect Jacques Moranne and the commanders of the gendarmerie brigades. So I came to warn Martine as soon as he told me.

Lucile enters the small living room. Martine and Second Lieutenant Billing were both sitting and drinking some kind of tea. Those who experienced this terrible period of war will be that it could not be called tea. It was more than bad in taste, but that's all you could get at the time. Martine looked at Lucile and understood that there was a problem. Martine stood up and said.

— What's going on Lucile?

— Loïc was arrested last night in Orleans by a patrol of the German army. And he drove him to the FeldKommandantur, rue de la République.

—It's not very good all that.

— That's not all! The Prefect and the Gendarmerie Commanders were summoned by the Germans.

— It's even worse. But what exactly did

he have to do in Orléans Loïc?

— He had to pretend to be a plumber and put a bomb in the building of the German General Staff, rue de la Bretonnerie. Lucile explains.

— Is it a problem if this person speaks? Ask Billing.

— If Loïc speaks, unfortunately many people will be arrested, tortured and then killed by the Germans.

—What do you want to do? Rescue him or kill him so that he does not speak? Request the Second Lieutenant.

—It must be taken out of the hands of the Germans. Lucile tries to see with your husband if the Germans made Loïc speak. And the information of the date of his transfer to the place where the Germans execute the French.

— Okay!

Shortly after the end of the conversation between Lucile, Martine and Second Lieutenant Billing, Laurent enters the room and is told.

— I have just received the reply from London.

Laurent gives Second Lieutenant Billing a sheet of paper where he had transcribed the message of the War Office. The Second Lieutenant reads the document and says.

— London asks that we do our mission

and that the idea of children for the collection of information be a good idea. They say that they themselves would not be suspicious of a young child who airs in the streets. Then for the extraction of everyone it will be necessary to do it in the free zone and this can only be done in several departures.

— So that's good news!

— But it would be necessary once our mission is over Martine that you and the members of your group come with us to London.

— Sorry, but I can't. I am French and my life is in my country.

— But what if you get captured?

— It is that it must unfold like this. It will be fate as they say.

— Lauren organizes the groups and look for how we can carry out our mission.

— Yes, my Lieutenant!

Lauren got to work. Lucile went home to wait for her husband who was due to return from the FeldKommandantur in Orleans. Cedric arrived and took the time to see Lauren.

— Hello Lauren, how are you?

— Hello, I'm fine thank you and yourself?

— I'm fine, but you know he doesn't have to want me. Do you have any news from London?

— They agreed. We would have to go and get children and my brother from the hiding place in Epieds-en-Beauce. My brother speaks French like me and so he can help us.

— I'll go straight to it.

Cedric overhears the conversation between Martine and Second Lieutenant Billing. He looks at Lauren and says in a low voice.

— What's going on?

— A person in your network was arrested tonight in Orleans. He wanted to plant a bomb at the German General Staff which is on the street I don't know what.

— Rue de la Bretonnerie?

— Yes, that right!

— Shit! Loïc! What a fool that one! I told him that his plan was stupid and more than risky.

—He wants to know what they can do to rescue him.

— There won't be much to do unfortunately. He will be tried and sentenced to death by the German court. Then a convoy will transport him for execution. Well, I'm going to get your brother and two or three kids to drive them here. But Loïc is more than stupid.

Disappointed by the news that Lauren has told him Cédric leaves the house and makes his way to Antoine's farm, the cousin of Lucile the wife of the Commander of the gendarmerie of Meung-sur-Loire.

Two hours later, Cedric is back at Martine's house accompanied by Lauren's older brother, Isaac and three children, including Simon. Cedric asks Martine to take a white sheet and stretch it. Lauren asks.

— Why make the white sheet?

— It is to take id photos to make them fake identity documents. I'm even going to make a fake police card for your big brother. This way the gendarmes of the sector will be afraid of him.

— Isaac smiled for the photo. Hey Lauren.

— No! Certainly not! It must seem a little sinister and unsociable, it will be much more realistic. Cédric explains.

— Yes, but the one and only picture I have left of him is in England at Ashford.

— Okay, I'll give you a picture of your big brother with a smile. Say Cedric.

At Cedric's words, Lauren rushed to him and kissed him on the cheeks. Isaac looks at the scene and says.

— But let's see! You French, I told you that I have your eye with my little sister.

— Isaac please be kind to him he saved my life.

— That's not a reason! If mom and dad were there. What would they say?

Lauren removed the arms she had placed around Cedric's neck and lowered her head and then she said.

— You're right, Isaac. They would say that it is not very elegant for a young woman to do this. Forgive me Cedric.

—It's nothing. It is a pleasure to be thanked from time to time. Well, we have to take the pictures now.

Cédric takes photographs of Isaac, Simon, Lucien, and Adrien. Then he opens his briefcase and takes out the documents. He entrusts the film of the camera to Martine so that she can proceed with the development of the photos. Twenty-five minutes later, the photographs were ready, and Cedric made the false identity documents. It was impressive to see him do it. Cédric was very focused on the production of his false papers.

— These are your new identity documents. You have to learn them by heart. And remember your new names and surnames. Your life depends on it! Cédric explains.

— So my name is now Grégorie Lafont! Say Isaac.

— That's right! Say Cedric.

— Okay, I think I'd remember it pretty easily.

Lucile comes back to Martine's house and says.

— Loïc didn't speak. He said he wanted revenge for his wife's death at the time of the great exodus when the Germans arrived. The German military court sentenced him to death, which will be done tomorrow morning at the Farm of Ormes. But the Germans executed thirty other people in retaliation for Loïc's attempted attack. And it is up to the Prefect to designate the thirty people who will be executed with Loïc tomorrow morning. The Gendarmerie Commanders must send the gendarmes to arrest the people this afternoon.

— But it's horrible! Lauren exclaims.

— This is the German method. Say Cedric.

Martine looks at Second Lieutenant Billing and tells him.

— Lieutenant, would you agree to help me set up a plan for the release of his unfortunates?"

— And how do we do it? There are not many of us for information. Say Second Lieutenant Billing.

— With other members of the network. Loïc is important to us. He has access to explosives. So you understand that you can't leave him without doing anything.

— Above all, it is necessary to identify the places. To then come up with a plan that holds up.

Two of the children came forward, and one of them, whose real name was Solomon known as Lucien said.

— We're going to come with you, it's going to be like a little family outing.

— It's too risky, young man. Say Billing.

— Sir, I have a question. Did my words seem like a question to you? I don't think so. That was a statement. You are not given a choice. It was just to inform you, period.

This is the first time I have seen someone standing up to Lieutenant Billing. Her children have courage and seem more than determined. This also surprises Second Lieutenant Billing who does not find a word to answer the child. Then, spending a little time the second child, Adrien continues the conversation.

— In addition to us, we know the sector more than you do. And most importantly, we are smarter than you. We Germans ignore us. While adults are always suspicious!

— Hey! I am an officer of King George VI. You think I became an officer by snapping my fingers?

— No, it had to be while drinking the tea.

— No, but oh! That's enough!

— Besides, you're old! Say Lucien.

— What I am only thirty-four years old!

— He's stupid or what they say he's old! Say Adrien.

— Well, well I don't talk to you anymore! Say Billing.

— Damn you upset the old one. The guys tell him you're sorry. Otherwise he will sulk. Say Simon.

— No, I'm not sulking!

— Okay... Forgive us the old one.

In the room everyone has a little smile. Finally almost everyone, Second Lieutenant Billing, he was not very satisfied to have to collaborate with the two young boys who had just made him turn into a mess.

The same afternoon Martine, Lucien, Adrien, and Second Lieutenant Billing leave with the car driven by Cédric towards the city of Orléans.

Cédric drops off the small group not far from the rue de la République. Martine, Lucien, Adrien, and Second Lieutenant Billing head towards the FeldKommandantur. A German patrol passes by them. The Second Lieutenant at their passage is feverish. He looks at Martine and tells her.

— We must monitor the place where they put your comrade.

— It must be rue de la Bretonnerie. Follow me.

The small group moves through the streets of the city. Whenever the group encounters German soldiers, it tries to recognize by their type of uniform and insignia their membership in Wehrmacht units.

Second Lieutenant Billing notes that there are also Panzer troops and Schutzstaffel troops. The Second Lieutenant knew that the troops of the Schutzstaffel were the group that was in charge of the massacres in Poland. The night before he had spoken through Lauren with the small group of Poles who were in Martine's basement. And that all its members were murderers. The Second Lieutenant wonders what his murderous troops are doing in the city of Orleans. Observing them, he understood that his troops were at rest. A rest before returning to the territories that Adolf Hitler wanted for his living space.

During the afternoon, the small group was able to count more than fifteen different German soldier divisions stationed in Orleans. It must be said that the city of Paris is about one hundred and thirty kilometers from this city. And that this city is also very close to the limit of the so-called free zone. The France during the Second World War was divided into two parts. The area occupied with Paris and covering a large part of the north and the west coast of the country and the free zone that covers the center and south of France.

The small group stands in front of a large building on Rue de la Bretonnerie. And Second Lieutenant Billing takes notes from a small notebook. He carefully notes the number of people entering and leaving the building, the schedules and guard points of the German sentries. The children and Martine take care of watching that no one approaches.

After two hours of their presence in this place, and those in a static way. A man in a suit darkens the remarks and begins to watch them for about ten minutes while smoking a cigarette. The man enters a building adjacent to the German General Staff building.

It was the headquarters of the French People's Party, which is the collaborationist movement. Suddenly men come out of this building and another building a little further. The small group was caught in a pincer. No possibility of escaping.

The men of the PPF catch Martine in first. Second Lieutenant Billing, seeing that Martine was being caught, rushed to try to free her. But four other men threw themselves at him. The men with batons beat the Lieutenant. Then, two groups of the PPF chase the children in the streets of Orleans. Lucien, the eldest of the two children, hides in a small alley behind a parked vehicle. Seeing that three men are coming towards him; he lies down and crawls under the vehicle. But unfortunately for him, a woman of a certain age, tells the men of the PPF where the child is hiding.

Adrien, despite the efforts of the men of the French People's Party, managed to escape them. He takes refuge in a courtyard of a building. The guard of this building seeing the young person sweating. He opens the door of his dressing room and makes him enter a small room.

— Quickly enter the cupboard, do not move, and especially do not say any words.

— Thank you, sir.

— Don't speak!

The man closed the cabinet door. And left with his broom to sweep in front of the building. He sees the four men of the PPF running in. The exhausted men look at the concierge of the building and one of them tells him.

— And you! Wouldn't you have seen a young boy running through here?

— No why!

— Are you certain morons?

— Of course I am sure yes. I would have seen it I clean the sidewalk of the building for more than fifteen minutes.

— Moron!

The four men of the PPF leave in the direction of the rue de la Bretonnerie.

Meanwhile, Martine, Lucien and Second Lieutenant Billing were taken to the premises of the French People's Party. The Second Lieutenant's face was bleeding. Martine she was holding her stomach following kicks that the men of the PPF had given her. Lucien kicked following the baton blows that a member of the PPF had sanitized him. All three were sitting on chairs in a small room of the building. One of the PPF men comes and tells them.

— Who are you?

— Go to hell! Lucien answers.

— Believe me young man hell will be for you in a few minutes.

— Don't touch the child! Say Martine.

— You don't worry your turn will come.

And I feel that we will have a lot of fun.

As he utters his words, the man touches Martine's face. The latter spits on the man. The man looks at her and then gives her a big slap. Second Lieutenant Billing seeing this, giggles and says.

— Aren't you ashamed to hit a woman?

The man approaches the Second Lieutenant and punches him twice in the face. Then he said to the Lieutenant.
— Personally, I don't mind hitting a woman. Especially if I think she's a dirty Jewish whore.

Shortly after two men, enter the room. Martine recognized the man who smoked his cigarette by observing them. The two men approach Lucien. And the greatest said to him.
— Go it's you who will have the honor to start!

At his words, the two men lift Lucien from his chair and take him with them. Lucien no longer touches the ground. But the latter squirms in all directions trying to free himself from the arms of the two men of the French Popular Party. The two men walk up a flight of stairs. They climb the two-story steps. They enter a room. And there, two other men were waiting for them. In the room there was a bathtub. Lucien told them.

— Do you want me to take a bath?

One of the men who were already in the room smiled and answered him.

— Yes of course, but only from your head. And besides, we will help you. Then you'll tell us what we want to know.

— I'm just a child. I don't know anything. Be a little smart it will change you. Oh forgive me it's true to do your job they recruit only fools.

— You'll see if we are fools!

On his words, the two men who held the young boy thirty centimeters above the ground, threw Lucien violently on the ground. Then another man approached and kicked the young man twice. The young boy made such a grimace that the pain was strong.

— Take him away!

The two men who had led Lucien into this torture room caught up with the young boy and placed him on a chair facing the bathtub. The tub was filled with water. This water was slightly tinged with red. Lucien looked at them and said.

— The water is not very transparent!

— It's the blood of the person who

passed here just before you! We'll get started.

Lucien guesses that, this carries a risk of being more than painful. But he has to hold on. Lucien told himself that the men of the French Popular Party had not managed to capture his friend Adrien. The young man hopes that his friend manages to return to Meung-sur-Loire and warn the other members of the house. Lucien does not know how long he will be able to last. But it will all do to last as long as possible.

The man approached Lucien and walked a hundred steps behind him. Then suddenly, he puts his right hand behind the young boy's head and makes him dive into the water of the bathtub. He immobilizes the head of the young man immersed in water for a minute. Then he brings Lucien's head out of the water.
— What is your name?
— Apple!

The man plunges the young boy's head back into the water for a minute and he says.
— What is your name?
— Orange!

The man plunges the boy's head back into the water for a minute and he repeats.
— You know I love my job. So I can do

this all day and even night. In your place, I would answer the question. So I'll do it again. What's your name?

— Go die a moron!

The man sighs and plunges the young Lucien's head back into the water this time for a minute and a half and he says.

— Believe me, if you want, but you're going to speak. They all do it! What is your name?

— Nobody!

The man plunges the young man's head back into the water again and while Lucien's head is in the water, he tells one of his colleagues.

— Go get me the marking iron of the animals in the chimney.

After a minute and thirty that Lucien's head is in the water. The man raises his head and asks him again.

— What is your name?

— I don't have a name!

The man smiled wide. He took the marking iron of the animals from the hands of his colleague and placed the glowing iron in the lower back of the young boy. At that moment, the pain gripped the young man who began to scream in pain. There was a horrible smell emanating from the room. Young Lucien was in tears due to the pain he had just suffered. The man asking the questions grabs Lucien's hair by pulling his head back. Then he whispers in her ear.

— Speak! Because it will continue for as long as it takes for me to know what I want to know. And believe me, I told you I love my job.

— Rather die than you speak! Say Lucien, moaning in pain.

— As you wish!

The man once again imposed the marking iron of the animals on the other side of the back of the young boy. Again, the young Lucien screams in pain.

German soldiers and officer with their sidecar.

7. IN PAIN.

It has been several hours since the young Lucien was interrogated by members of the French People's Party. As soon as the young man fainted, the members of the PPF woke him up by throwing ice water on his back marked with a red iron.

A man from the party of collaboration with the Germans comes down and he tells Martine.

— You are next. We'll soon be done with the child!

— You are monsters... You are attacking a child.

On her words, the young woman spat in the face of the man collaborating with the German invader. The man stared at Martine, then wiped the spit on her face. He walked towards the young and frail woman and then punched her first in the face, then he put a second punch in the stomach. The man said to her with a smile.

— I'm sure I'll have a lot of fun with you. In addition, you are not ugly as a spy. Believe me when I'm done with you... You'll talk... I would even say, you will sing... For you, I would try, and I am sure you will love to have me in you.

The man starts laughing out loud. Then he comes out of the room and calls two of his colleagues and tells them.

— Take her to office 210! I will take care of her personally and I am sure I will have a great time. I think she is overdressed. When she is in the office, please make her feel comfortable and take off her clothes.

— At your command! one of the two men replies.

Martine looks at the man with a look of contempt and disgust. The two men grabbed the young woman, and he made her climb the steps two by two. They arrive on the landing of the second floor of the building. One of the two men opens the door to the right of the stairs. The door gives on a long corridor of several offices. One of the two men of the French People's Party pushed

Martine to advance in the corridor. They pass by closed doors. Suddenly, Martine sees an open door. And she sees the young boy who had accompanied them. He was on the ground. It seemed inert. But a man in the room kicked him in the stomach. She heard the young Lucien groan in pain at the violence of the blow. She noticed his back which had been marked by many repetitions by the hot iron. But the worst thing was the smell. The smell of burnt human flesh. It is a smell that people who have experienced this sad period and who have experienced the interrogation sessions cannot forget.

The two collaborators stopped in front of the door where the young Lucien was, and both laughed. Then one of them said to Martine.

— This is what awaits you! It's a lot of fun. And that's the part of our work that we prefer. Believe me.

— Normal for cowards and traitors like you. You like to hit women and children. It makes you feel like a real man. But a day will come when men like you will pay for it.

On his words one of the two men punched the young woman in the face. He struck so hard that Martine fell to the ground. The man told her.

— And that's just the beginning. Believe

me.

One of the men grabbed Martine's hair and dragged her to the ground. Martine screamed in pain. When he arrived at the door of office 210, the man let go of the young woman's hair. But in his hand, there was a tuft of the latter's hair. The second man opened the door of the office, he grabbed Martine and raised her. Then he pushes the young woman violently inside the room.

The room resembles most interrogation pieces. There was a chair, a bathtub, a fireplace, and a desk. In accordance with the instructions they had received from the first man. One of the men put his hand at the top of the collar of the young woman's dress. Then with a violent gesture, he pulled his hand down. This gesture made the seams of Martine's dress crack and made her appear the chemise that the young woman wears under what was a beautiful dress of a blueberry flower print.

Martine was sad because she remembered that it was her late husband who had given her this dress just a fortnight before the Germans arrived in the Loiret department. The man, who appears to be the leader of the other two, enters the office. He approaches the young woman and tells her.

— I see that you have put yourself at ease.

I am delighted.

— You are just dirty pigs.

— Let's see, dirty Jew... We are not pigs. And I feel that you will appreciate what I have in store for you.

— You are only drafts! In your place I would be ashamed!

— Friends... Question... Are you ashamed of our work for the Marshal?

— Of course not! It is a pride to do our job for the Marshal! one of the two men replies.

— Dirty vermin!

— Please be polite!

— Gang of cowards!

— Let me introduce myself...

— I don't care about your dirty name traitor!

— I'm Aristide LEOPOLE!

— One day you will pay for it...

— Who will make us pay? You?

— No DE GAULLE and the English.

— Germany will conquer England and the English will submit to Germany so the English will do nothing to us.

— That's what we'll see!

The man begins to turn around the young woman. Striking in his hand with a cow. All while turning around Martine, he looks at her insistently. And he said to her.

— Too bad you're a big Jewish slut. I admit that you are very cute in your little outfit.

At his words he placed the leather strap of the cow between Martine's buttocks and began to raise the young woman's chemise. The young woman takes a step to the side.

— Let's see little Jewish girl... We could both have fun. I can be very gentle, you know.

— You're just a big, disgusting pig!

The man on the words of the young woman puts a whip on her knee joint. This blow makes Martine bend her knees.

"The child refuses to tell us who you are and why you are here. But I suspect that you are spies in the pay of the Judeomasonic conspiracy.

— We were visiting the city.

— Do you see that? You visit the city of Orleans at our offices. That's fun!

— Yes, I swear!

— And when you visit, you write down on a notebook the places where the Germans are in place. You are strange anyway.

— We didn't do anything wrong.

— We don't hurt people either. And I even went further by saying that women have their facts only good. Say the man with a broad smile.

— Well, not with me!

— Tell me who you are! And who is the

man who is with you?

 — He's a German.

 — Do you think we are idiots?

 — Of course you do!

The man punched the young and delicate Martine. He makes a wide smile, and he says.

 — It feels good. I particularly like hitting people. It relaxes me. Despite the fact that there are so many ways to relax with a woman.

 — Go to hell! Dirty traitor!

 — Let's see we could do good to each other.

Martine spits in his face again. The angry man shoves her. The young woman is on the ground and the man kicks her in the stomach. After about twenty kicks in the stomach, the man takes the iron that was installed in the embers of the chimney. He walks up to Martine and tells her.

 — You're going to be marked like what we do to animals. After all you are a big Jewish sow. And you're lucky youpine that I haven't put a bullet in your head yet.

As a result of his words, the man repeatedly pushed the cattle iron on Martine's body. The latter screamed in pain. The iron had been made with the shape of the PPF emblem. The man marked his lower back in the spine. He marked the young woman on her chest and legs, but he did not stop there the last two marks he wanted them at the level of the posterior of the young woman. Each time, let him impose the burning iron on poor Martine scream and beg him to stop.

The man leaves to rest the iron that had taken shreds of flesh from the young woman in the glowing embers. The man comes back to Martine and tells her.

— Are you going to talk? Or do we start again?

— No... Stop I'll talk.

— Well... That's great. Say the man, caressing the young woman's head.

— But promise me to release the child. He has nothing to do with it and he knows absolutely nothing.

— I promise you that once you tell us everything you will be able to see the child.

— You promise me?

— I have only one word. I promise you will see the child. He will come here.

— Okay... I tell you all.

The man signaled the other two members of the French People's Party to pick up the young woman and sit her in the chair. Then during this time he walks to the office and sits on it.

— Tell me your identity?

— My name is Martine Delporte, I live in Meung-sur-Loire. I help a group of English parachuting a few days ago collected information on the positions of the German troops present in the area.

— The man who is with you is an Englishman?

— Yes, but I don't know his real name.

— How many are the English?

— It's a small group... There are only three of them.

— And what were the children's roles?

— Children serve as a blanket. They don't know anything about the group or the plan.

— Is this lie true?

— I tell you the truth! Children have nothing to do with history.

— Okay... Do you want to see the child?

— Yes please.

— Sebastian... Go get us the child.

— All of them right away boss!

The man leaves the room and three minutes later he returns with the young Lucien. They both walk into the room. The man who was sitting on the desk gets up and stands behind Lucien and he says.

— You see Martine... I keep my promise... the young man is there in the same room as you.

— Lucien, are you okay?

— I've had better days and...

Lucien had not finished his sentence that the man of the French Popular Party had taken out his gun and shot him in the head from behind. The young boy collapsed on the ground. And a pool of blood begins to come out of his skull. The young woman starts screaming.

— NO... Why did you kill him?

— He was a spy, you told us.

— You said you'd let him go if I tell you all!

— I never said that Martine... I just promised you that the boy would be in the room with you. He was a spy in the pay of the British. It's impossible to let him come out alive.

— That's not true... What did I do...

— You made the right choice... Martine... He had chosen his side. Unfortunately for him it was not the victors' camp and neither mine. He had to die. It was inevitable.

It was on this day that the young Lucien of his real name Salomon Rosemblum died in office number 210 of the headquarters of the French Popular Party of Orleans which is located in the rue de la Bretonnerie. The young Solomon had left Belgium with his parents at the time of the invasion of German troops. Both his parents were killed by a Messerschmitt BF109, during the great exodus on French territory near the city of Beaune la Rolande. And in the days following his parents' death, he met other orphaned children like him. And together he was only looking to survive.

The man approached the young woman. He leaned towards her. And he said to her, whispering in her ear.

— Don't worry... You and the Englishman will soon join him. I promise you. And you know now that I always keep my promises, Martine.

— You are repugnant! I curse you dirty traitor.

— It's not nice Martine to tell me that... I scrupulously respected what I promised you and now you blame me. That's not nice of you.

— One day you will have to be accountable to the French people and your life will be over. It's a shame that I may not be there to see him anymore otherwise I would be happy to relieve myself on your grave.

— Martine... I will give you some information. Your English spy friend and you will return a small visit to our friends of the Kommandantur. You will see they are very nice.

— Dirty collaborator rat!

The man sketches a broad smile. Then he

stares at the young woman and says without even looking at his colleague.

— Go get the Englishman and put the irons on the wrists of the Jewish slut.

— All immediately-chef!

Without waiting, one of the men leaves the room while the second puts Martine in handcuffs. Then he takes her by the arms and takes her out of the room. The young woman passing by the inert body of the young child, she looks away. In the corridor two other men were waiting to be interrogated by the PPF. Martine looked at their faces. But the collaborating man pushed her forward. The young woman drags her feet to do everything not to go to the Kommandantur. Because she knew the Germans were going to sentence them to death. At the top of the stairs, the young woman struggles not to go down the steps. But the man of the Collaboration Party had decided otherwise and so he decided to push Martine down the stairs. The young woman finds herself at the bottom of the steps when the second man arrives with Second Lieutenant Billing. The Englishman asks Martine.

"Are you okay? Didn't you hurt yourself too much? You have blood all over you.

— No, it wasn't on the stairs that I did that to myself.

— I spoke... I am sorry... I thought I

would save Lucien's life... But his big pigs were slaughtered like a dog. I am sorry...

— WE DON'T TALK! Come on English we will see people who would like to see you.

— Oh well, are you going to take me to see your wife?

— No! It's too funny the British!

— No, I know it's your mother... But you know I prefer young women. The old ones don't interest me at all. I have trouble going to bed with the old ones.

— WE'RE SILENT! Otherwise I do you the same fate as the young idiot who was with you... Do you understand Rosbif?

— Hector! You won't do anything about it the Germans will want it alive. At least for now...

The small group leaves the building of the French People's Party and heads towards the FeldKommandantur. Arriving in front of the guard in his booth one of the two men of the PPF said.

— We have a client for you it would be necessary to hand it over to the Obersleutnant der Polizei Hans Grüber. He is an English paratrooper and a spy who is suspected of being a Jew.

— Just a moment.

The guard soldier turns to his colleague and speaks to him in German. His colleague immediately runs towards the building. A few minutes later, about twenty German soldiers and an officer came out of the building and came to meet the two members of the collaborators. Seeing this, Second Lieutenant Billing scoffs.

— All his soldiers just for the two of us. Well, they must be afraid that we have a tank in our pocket.

— But you're going to keep quiet Rosbif?

— Sorry you mean something.

— But it's not true he's not going to be silent this andouille!

The German officer speaking French with a very strong Germanic accents says.

— You managed to capture the British paratrooper terrorists. But congratulations the sincerest. We will take care of it. It will be fast.

— Thank you and believe me we trust you completely to take care of their cases. Delighted to have been able to collaborate with you to destroy The Judeomaconsian plots.

The German soldiers supervise the young Martine and the Second Lieutenant Billing. And the group enters the courtyard of the building. Meanwhile the two men of the French People's Party return to their buildings. Soldiers and prisoners enter the FeldKommandantur building. Arriving in the lobby to enter it, finding an office with two guards armed with machine guns and a kind of reception secretary. In front of the double door called, à la Française, there is a staircase and at the top of the staircase a large red vertical banner with a white circle with a large swastika in its center. The people already present in the building look at the young Martine and the Second Lieutenant Billing. Second Lieutenant Billing told the young woman to frighten.

— I think his Germans have never seen a Brit in their lives. I feel like a circus animal.

The young woman makes a slight nervous laugh. The German officer said.

— The Englishman with me! The Jewish woman remains in the corridor of the west wing.

— They must be stupid his Germans they think I'm Jewish.

The officer heard Martine's words and turned to her and told her.

— You're not Jewish?

— Of course not! I am just a patriot who refuses collaboration with you!

— The true French patriots are with the German Reich Madame!

— No, the true French patriots are with General de GAULLE! And will always be against the German invaders! And the France remains a great nation thanks to DE GAULLE, and we will always resist Nazi fascists like you!

— You are just a terrorist under the rule of the English. Your soldiers and your Marshal Pétain surrendered. Germany is a great nation!

Second Lieutenant Billing laughs. One of the soldiers next to him kicks his stomach with a rifle butt. Billing following the blow of the rifle butt carried by the German soldier puts a knee on the ground.

The Officer signals four of the soldiers to take the Second Lieutenant to an office. Then the Officer said to the young woman.

— Don't worry! I will be back to you shortly.

Then the Officer joins Second Lieutenant Billing in the room. One of the soldiers makes Billing sit.

The German officer stands on a chair in front of the latter.

— If we start with your identity? Who are you?

— Second Lieutenant Billing... Number 2451256... Company of Riffles Guard of His Majesty King George VI.

— What is your mission?

— Second Lieutenant Billing... Number 2451256... Company of Riffles Guard of His

Majesty King George VI.

— I know that... I asked you what your mission is.

— Second Lieutenant Billing... Number 2451256... Company of Riffles Guard of His Majesty King George VI.

— I see you don't want to tell me what the purpose of your mission is?

— Second Lieutenant Billing... Number 2451256... Company of Riffles Guard of His Majesty King George VI.

— Yes... Yes... Yes... I know Billing... Number and thing of the king... Question Lieutenant do you really want us to question your friend the woman?

— Second Lieutenant Billing... Number 2451256... Company of Riffles Guard of His Majesty King George VI.

— SS-Obersturmführer Ditrich!

— Yes Obersleutnant?

— Go get me the woman!

— At your orders Obersleutnant!

The soldier comes out of the office and grabs the young woman by the arm. Martine tries to struggle, but nothing helps the German is stronger than her and manages to drag her to the office where Second Lieutenant Billing is. The Officer snaps his fingers and signals that she must sit down.

— Madam... Tell me what your friend the British spy is called.

— How do you want me to know... They've been here for barely a week!... And you're not very smart you tell me... You do not know that for security we do not know the real name and surname of each other?

— How so? How many are you? How many Englishers are there?

— At home I don't know the number. But the English are at least three hundred.

— SS-Obersturmführer make sure all immediately call Berlin and tell the General Staff that there are according to our sources between three hundred and four hundred British soldiers hiding in the area. We need reinforcements and quickly we do not know what they want. And please summon the commander of the DCA right away... I have questions for him. He said they saw that 4 parachutes... I wonder if the soldiers of the DCA know how to count! They must have Jewish blood to be so stupid.

The Officer looked insistently at Second Lieutenant Billing and said to him.

— What is your mission?

— Second Lieutenant Billing... Number 2451256... Company of Riffles Guard of His Majesty King George VI.

— I see you still don't want to talk!

However you want!

— According to the Geneva Convention, I must give my name, rank, number and body of arms and nationality.

— Yes, but you are a spy!

— No, I am a soldier of His Majesty King George VI.

— Guard! Take his two prisoners to the basement.

The guards raise Second Lieutenant Billing and young Martine from their chairs. Then they make them leave the office and take them downstairs. Arriving in front of a door a guard opens the door which leaves a dark and damp corridor in front of them.

They move the two prisoners forward and a guard stops in front of a door and opens it. And he says.

— The woman has it in it!

And he pushes Martine. And the door closes behind her. Then the guard opens the docking cell and says.

— You English here!

And he in turn pushes the Second Lieutenant into the cell and then locks the door. Lieutenant Billing saw in a corner at the bottom of his cell an air vent that overlooked the young woman's cell. He approaches and says.

— Martine, can you hear me?

— Yes, I hear you, Lieutenant!

— Do you have a bed or mattress in your cell?

— No, my Lieutenant!

— Me neither! Why did you say that we were three hundred British soldiers in the area.

— You didn't understand my Lieutenant? German soldiers sought four British paratroopers. Now German soldiers are looking for between three hundred and four hundred soldiers. They had a very long time to do so before they found the three hundred to four hundred British soldiers. I wish them courage.

— It's sure to look for troops that don't exist is a bit complicated. And I feel that they will yell at each other about it, camping each of the sections on their positions. The DCA with their four parachutes and you who tell the Kommandantur that there are several hundred soldiers. On the other hand, I hope that the young boy was able to go home to warn them of what happened. And I hope they will take shelter in a safe place.

Emblem of the People's Party French (P.P.F)
Founded and led by Jacques Doriot, was the main fascist-inspired
political party French in 1936-1939 and one of the two main
collaborationist parties in 1940-1944, along with the Rassemblement
National Populaire (RNP) of Marcel Déat.

8. DEATH AT THE TURN.

Only a few hours have passed, since the young Martine and Second Lieutenant Billing were locked in their cell by the Germans of the FeldKommandantur. Sounds of boots echo in the corridor in front of the cells.

This is when the doors of the two cells open. The German soldier takes out Martine and Second Lieutenant Billing. The two prisoners of the Germans climb the steps and lead him back into the Obersleutnant's office. Two guards are already in the office and the German police officer is behind his desk. The guard who leads the prisoners makes them sit down by leaning on their shoulders. The Obersleutnant stares at the young woman and Lieutenant Billing. After two minutes of silence. Silence that seemed to the frail young woman like an eternity. The German officer spoke.

— How was your night among us, tell me?

— Personally, I have known better and the service leaves something to be desired if you want my opinion. Second Lieutenant Billing explains.

— Yes, I agree with him. I have never seen such a deplorable service.

— What? No, but what is his remarks? Know that we are not here to take care of you! You are prisoners of the army of the German Third Reich. You are not at the hotel here!

— Still happy, otherwise I would refuse to pay the bill. We weren't even placed a square of chocolate on our pillow. Billing reply.

— I think I know why, my Lieutenant... There were no pillows in the cells.

— Enough is enough! You are prisoners!

— I think the German army thought it was a big army! But we see here that it is mediocre. She didn't even receive guests in their buildings. Continue Billing.

— It's true that a small piece of chocolate is always a pleasure. But you know Lieutenant Billing, the Germans are not known for their hospitality and their savoir-vivre. They are not like the British and French people who have a very high level of hospitality culture. And who know how to receive people!

— You are not my guests here! You are just prisoners!

— Oh well, that's how you take it Obersleutnant? Mrs. Martine, since they do not consider us as guests... We're leaving! I have never seen such rude hosts!

— I am a Lieutenant to you!

The young woman and Second Lieutenant Billing get up and begin to walk towards the office door. The soldier who was behind them hurries to position himself in front of the door to block their passage.

— Please sit down! Say Obersleutnant.

— It's a big deal! We are asked to sit down while the service is more than deplorable!

— You are prisoners! What do you not understand in the term that you are prisoners?

— Okay then I tell you that from now on I refuse to talk to you! Billing retorts.

— You're going to talk! Believe me!

— That's right... I would tell my horse about it!

— What? Which horse are you talking about Lieutenant?

— No, I don't talk to you anymore! I make your head. And I wouldn't say anything anymore. Pig who renounces it.

— What? But which pig? I don't understand anything you say Lieutenant!

The young woman looks at the German officer and starts laughing.

— Why are you laughing, ma'am?"

— I laugh because he tells you typical French expressions and you don't understand anything! You who say that the Germans are the greatest, the most beautiful and the most cultured. He has just shown, you the opposite.

— Lieutenant! Are you kidding me?

Second Lieutenant Billing did not answer the German officer's question.

— Lieutenant! I asked you a question!

Billing does not answer. But the latter makes a smile.

— Lieutenant! I order you to answer my question! Are you making fun of me?

Still no answer from Second Lieutenant Billing. Martine laughs more beautifully and then she pronounces the following words.

— So... You... You must be particularly stupid!

— What? How dare you insult an officer of the German army, madam?

— It's very simple as I just did! But let me explain, please.

— In addition, you admit?

— Well... I'm not going to lie to you... You already look pretty stupid like that! But let me explain... The Lieutenant told you that he doesn't talk to you anymore... So he does what he said... And if you don't understand it, it's because you're stupid!

— But it's not up to him to decide whether he's talking to me or not! I am an officer in the great army of the Third Reich! I'm Obersleutnant! He owes me respect! When I ask a question... I am told it's an order!

— Tell me if I'm wrong... Obersleutnant is the equivalent of Second Lieutenant or Second Lieutenant?

— Yes... Tell me what the problem is.

— You didn't, see?

— No! I ask a question... They have to answer me! That's an order! I don't see why he doesn't obey one of my orders!

— Oh my god... How stupid that one is! First, Obersleutnant, you have the same rank! Secondly, you are not in the same army! So your order you can put it, or I think!

— What? I don't understand!

— I suspected that you don't understand much. But to put it simply and to make sure you understand me, I'll explain it to you in very simple terms... Your order... You can put it in your ass! In the ass the praline!

— How dare you talk to me in this way?

— I have to use very simple words for you to understand. Question on the day of brain distribution... You were absent because the conversation goes in circles.

The German officer begins to see red because he realizes that the young woman and Second Lieutenant Billing were making fun of him by placing insults in their words.

— You're starting to me off both of you!

— It's not nice to say that! I try to explain things to you so that you don't seem to be more stupid than you all are in the German army. In particular, the dwarf with the small mustache that is in photography behind you! Besides, it's ugly! Want people to have nightmares when they see his psychopath's head?

— Who are you talking about?

— The moron with the mustache behind you! In the photograph.

The officer turns around and looks at the photograph that the young woman is talking about and realizes that Martine is talking about German Chancellor Adolf Hitler. He turns to the prisoners and says in a loud voice.

— You're talking about our Führer! Our Führer is not a psychopath as you say! And he's not a moron! Thanks to him, we dominate a very large part of Europe and soon the world!

— Well... You seem to me to be one of the most confident Obersleutnant!

— Madam... Is it the French who are in Germany or the Germans who are in France? Oh! Pardons... I forgot that there are French people in Germany... Prisoners all like both of you... German soldiers at your home!... The French Soldiers at home!

— Yes, because you fear that the people of France will set our husbands, sons, and brothers free... But do you know that this is contrary to the Geneva Convention?

— And who is going to stop us? You?

— No, the International Red Cross!

— The Swiss are very afraid of us. In two days, we could occupy the whole of Switzerland. They will do nothing. They are cowards all like the French officers who hid when the great army of the Third Reich advanced like a tank without brakes.

At this time, a person knocks on the door of the office. The Obersleutnant looks at the door and says.

— Yes... Come in!

He was another officer in the German army. The Obersleutnant stares at him and tells him.

—What do you want? You didn't see that I'm with prisoners right now?

— Obersleutnant... You were the one who sent your assistant to tell me that you want to see me.

— No, it's not possible!... I never gave that order!... In fact, I do not know who you are!...

— I am Hauptmann Ludwig Von Strässer.

— That doesn't tell me anything!... Get out now!

— I am the commander of the DCA Ouest Loiret.

— I don't remember! Exit! ...

The young woman starts laughing again. Seeing her laugh, Second Lieutenant Billing laughed in turn. The Obersleutnant turns to them and says.

— Why are you both still laughing?

— Because in addition to being stupid you are Alzheimer's.

— What? ...

— Yesterday before you took us down to the cells below. By the way, I take this opportunity to remind you that I want a square of chocolate on my pillow. You told another moron in the German army to summon the head of the DCA.

— You are prisoners! There will be no

chocolate on the pillows... Besides, you don't even have pillows in your cells!

— Yes, by the way, we should talk about it again. It would take pillows so that you can put a square of chocolate on it every day.

— Madam, what do you not understand in the sentence?... You are prisoners, so no pillows and therefore, no chocolate!

— Okay, we'll talk about it again later.

— No! We won't talk about it again today... Nor tomorrow...

— Okay, so we'll talk about it again the day after tomorrow. But be careful I note that you owe us the three chocolates each. One for yesterday evening, one for today and one for tomorrow.

— No chocolate! And we'll never talk about it again! Have you understood correctly now?

The Obersleutnant turns to the Hauptmann and tells him.

— It is because of his two individuals that I have summoned you to our offices!

— How does two people concern the DCA Ouest Loiret Obersleutnant?

— Oh, but it's very simple Hauptmann! The man is British, and he is one of the men who jumped on your protection zone!

— Is he one of the four paratroopers?

— Hauptmann! They said he is part of a group of three hundred to four hundred soldiers!

— It's impossible they were only four jumped from the plane we shot down!

— Yes, well that means that either paratrooper jumped without your knowledge. Which would make you incompetent wherever you lied in your report!

— How dare you Obersleutnant! I have been a soldier of the Reich since I am certain much longer than you! My family has been serving the German army for many, many years since you were not yet born!

— There are British paratrooper commandos on our sector and if they are between three hundred and four hundred it poses a heavy problem Hauptmann!

— Have you ever thought that they gave you three hundred to four hundred paratroopers to disturb you?

— What?

— I say do you believe his British or a German artillery officer who also has many decorations awarded by Generals Wilhelm Keitel and Alfred Jodl? Tell me Obersleutnant?

— That's right... That would make a lot of British soldiers on the area.

— Obersleutnant... Know that I pass this time on your accusations about my duty as an officer. But know that if it happens again. I would report directly to my staff.

— Excuse me... But you will understand that this information was disturbing.

— I certainly understand it... But never question my word or my reports again!

— Understood Hauptmann Von Strässer!

— Can I dispose now?

— Yes, Hauptmann Von Strässer! Happy end of the day Hauptmann Von Strässer!

— Heil Hitler!

— Heil Hitler! Hauptmann Von Strässer.

Hauptmann Von Strässer came out of the room. The Obersleutnant turns to the young woman and Second Lieutenant Billing. He didn't look very happy. He stares at them for a minute without saying a word. Then he said.

— You!

Second Lieutenant Billing points his index finger at him.

— Yes!! You!! Through your fault, I may have very big problems! And if I have very big problems... Imagine the very big problems you would also have!

—He did absolutely nothing or say anything.

— What?

— Then you, you should consult a doctor as soon as possible. He was not the one who told you that they were between three and four hundred British paratroopers.

— Oh yes, so who is it?

— That's me! But it is an approximation that I was communicating to you. That is not to say that my numbers are perfectly accurate. After if you get excited about approximations this is not my problem, but it is yours.

— Admit it! You want me dead!

— Personally, and this only binds me. I would never allow myself to speak on behalf of Second Lieutenant Billing. I don't know you well enough to want you dead. But since you are German, and you refuse to give me a pillow with a square of chocolate a day. I think that might make me want you dead. Well I agree with you just the fact that you are German make me want your death.

— Certainly, I can conceive of it. But I hope you can imagine that I will have you transferred to one of our prisons in Germany!

— If you want! It doesn't scare me!

The officer turns to his aide-de-camp and tells her.

— SS-Obersturmführer Ditrich!

— Yes Obersleutnant?

— Please return the prisoners to their respective cells.

— At your orders Obersleutnant!

The Obersleutnant's aide-de-camp signaled the three guards to take the prisoners to their cells under his responsibility.

In the meantime, the young Adrien had managed to return to Martine's house. Seeing the very young boy return alone, without Martine or Second Lieutenant Billing, the members of the British commando understand that the mission was a failure and that the other members of the mission left for the city of Orleans were captured by the Germans.

—What happened? Lauren asks.

— We were spotted by the members of the PPF, and they attacked us.

— What is PPF?

— It's the French People's Party, they're traitors and collaborators with the Germans.

— But they caught everyone?

— I don't know. For sure, they caught Martine and the Lieutenant. For Lucien I don't know when we fled, we separated. I was lucky a concierge of a building hiding me at home. I came out only at nightfall. And I walked trying to avoid the German and French patrols.

— If they have been captured, it is not very good to stay here. We have to leave the house as soon as possible!

— I'm not making you say.

Lauren calls the radio operator Laurent and tells him.

— Martine and probably Lieutenant Billing were captured by men named PPF and as far as Lucien is concerned, Adrien has no news they have not managed to stay together.

— You say the men of the PPF?

— Yes!

—It's not very good all that. I will tell you General De Gaulle says that the PPF has communicated secret information to the services of the Abwehr. And to be honest, the Germans knew far too much information about our radio codes and our units. They are fascists even before the beginning of the war. They even organized campaigns against the entry into the war of the France against the Germans.

— In short, you mean they are traitors?

— Yes!... And if the Lieutenant and Martine are their prisoners, they will suffer before being handed over to the Germans!

— We should leave here and take everyone with us. What do you think Laurent?

—Leaving is a no-brainer! But I wonder how we will manage to get everyone out and especially where we could go.

— Cedric must pass in the morning. We're going to ask him. He will know how to do it!

A few minutes after Adrien's arrival, Cedric hurriedly returns to the house.

— Martine and Second Lieutenant Billing were delivered to the Germans of the FeldKommandantur.

— And Lucien do you know if he has been captured. Lauren asks.

— Lucien was killed during his interrogation by a PPF man.

— My god. That's terrible.

— You have to leave the place! And now! I had the information that the men of the PPF and the Germans are coming here!

— But how do we do for the Poles in the cellar? And where are we going to hide?

— I have another place far from Meung-sur-Loire. There, you will be safe!

— But Martine and Second Lieutenant Billing are alive?

— Yes, they are alive... At least... For now!

— We can't help them?

— No! This is far too dangerous! And I don't want to lose another person. Do you understand Lauren?

—Yes, I understand.

The small group begins to gather their belongings. And to bring up from the cellar the group of Polish Jews. Five minutes later, a truck arrives on the street. Lauren begins to get scared thinking it's the Germans. But in fact, it is Armand the cousin of Lucile the wife of the commander of the gendarmerie of Meung-sur-Loire who has just arrived. Armand was not alone, with him three other men whose size and corpulence were well above the norm. Armand in turn returns to the house, while the other two men watch the street where Martine's house is located.

— Ready to go? asks the colossus.

— Yes, we are almost ready, it is just missing to take things for Martine's son.

—Well... Because we have to act quickly. The men of the PPF and the Germans can arrive from one moment to the next!

— Don't worry Armand, I asked members of the network to post themselves on several points and when they arrive, they will have a surprise. Believe me!

— This will make them foot on his dirty traitors of the PPF and his dirty boches! And my cousin's husband told me he will try to hold them back as well.

— That's it all ready. Hey Lauren.

— Perfect! Here we go! We take the Poles out and everyone will carry two suitcases! And everyone will have to take a gun just in case. You never know enough to have bad luck. It is better to plan. Cédric explains.

— Then we go to the truck in groups of four. In four times, it will be done like this!

— Yes, you're right... We can't all go out at the same time... To go out one by one would be much too long and therefore dangerous...

The people present in Martine's house, that day looks at each other. We see grandparents kissing their children and grandchildren as if they were not going to see each other again or like this they were all going to die. This scene will remain forever in my memory.

— Come on!! Are you ready?... Here we go! Good luck to all!

The first group consisted of the grandparents and four grandchildren of the Polish group. He rushed in and the two men helped them get into the tarpaulin truck.

Three minutes later, it was the turn of the parents and five other children to leave the house. They also get into the truck.

A few minutes later, it is a group composed of five women, two girls and Armand, Lucile's cousin and the resistance fighter who hide in his farm other people who leave Martine's house and get into the truck.

Finally, the group composed of Lauren, Laurent, Cédric and Lucas, Martine's son comes out of the house, but they head to Cédric's car. Cedric before getting in the car turns to Armand and tells him.

— You know where you need to go! I say good luck, my friend! And long live the Free France!

— Good luck to you too! And yes... Long live France!

Cedric begins to leave in the direction of the new place where we have to hide from the men of the PPF and the Germans.

We had left Martine's house less than a minute ago when suddenly we hear the sounds of weapons. I turned around and saw the men in the truck and Armand pulling out the guns in their hands and shooting at something. Personally, I suspect that Armand and his two friends are shooting at PPF men or Germans who arrive at street level where Martine's house is located.

— We're not going to rescue them?

— No, it's too dangerous for you!

— But they are going to be slaughtered!

— When we enter the resistance, it is for an ideal and we know it we can die, and that Armand and the others are aware of it.

I turn around and see one of the men who was with Armand fallen to the ground. A few moments later, I see Armand, this giant fallen in turn. Then a few seconds later, when Armand falls to the ground, the truck explodes.

You may tell me it's because I'm a woman. But I confess to you that at that time. The sadness of seeing people I met during the time I was in Martine's house made me cry. At that moment, Cédric took out of the inner pocket of his jacket a handkerchief and gave it to me.

— Wipe your eyes... It makes me sad when you cry. I'd rather see you laugh.

Meanwhile, at the gendarmerie brigade of Meung-sur-Loire, men of the PPF enter in numbers accompanied by German soldiers.

At the guard, it is the gendarme Belleville who for reminder had been punished by the Commander of the Brigade during the visit of Lauren and Cédric. Constable Belleville says.

— Hello gentlemen, how can I help you?

— We are looking for English paratroopers who would be hidden in your city.

— English paratroopers?? Just that!

— Gendarme we're not kidding! We captured a British officer yesterday afternoon in Orleans near our buildings and near the

FeldKommandantur!
>   — Is that true?
>   — Of course it's true! Do you think we come to see the muddies for our pleasure?
>   — Well, know that I would help you all. But here, you see I have to stay here. And my superior and angry because I mistreated Jews so I'm how to say... Punished!
>   — And your Jews, where are they now?
>   — He released them!
>   — What? But your Commander is completely stupid or what?
>   — Go get it for us.
>   — At your command!

Constable Belleville leaves the station of the brigade guard and goes to look for the Commander in his office. In the Commander's office, there is his wife, Lucile. And Constable Belleville told him.
>   — Commander of the men asks to see you!
>   — And who are his men in question gendarme Belleville?
>   — They are men of the PPF accompanied by German soldiers.

The Commander leaves his office accompanied by his wife and Constable Belleville. The Commander asks.

— What can I do to serve you?

— We are looking for English paratroopers.

— Yes, I heard about it from the Prefect Jacques Moranne, during our meeting at the Kommandantur.

— Yesterday afternoon, we arrested one of the members of this British commando. And we know that they are on this sector, more than with him, there was a woman who told us that they were in your city!

— What?

— Where are his Englishmen and where are the youpins that this gendarme arrested?

— There are no Englishmen in our cells and for the Jews I reminded them of the law not to enter public places and then I released them!

— I don't like it commander! I don't like it at all! You and your lady will accompany us to our offices. Gendarme the time of the absence of your senior officer you will take command of the Brigade. And your first mission is to search all, I mean all the houses on the Meung-sur-Loire sector!

— At your command!

The Commander and his wife Lucile were escorted by German soldiers and four men from the PPF. The members of the PPF put them in the back of a derailed truck. Then the truck makes its way towards the city of Orléans.

Constable Belleville rings the gathering of the brigade. After five minutes that all the gendarmes are, gather. He speaks up and says.

— Gentlemen, I replace the Commander of the Brigade for the time of his absence! The men of the PPF and the German soldiers, present here, ask us to reinforce them in the hunt for the British commando who came killed French and Germans on our territory! So our duty, and as Marshal Pétain wants, is to defend and protect the France against the troops sent to our soil by officers under the influence of Judeo-Masonic groups. So, gentlemen... Hunting!

At the end of this speech the gendarmes, members of the PPF and the German soldiers leave the gendarmerie brigade and begin to search the houses of the city of Meung-sur-Loire.

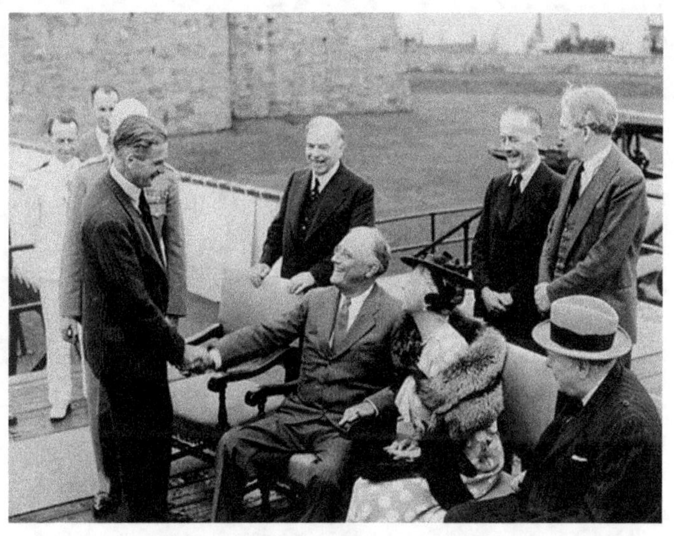

Anthony Eden (initiator of the Light in the Night Project) serves the hand of American President Franklin D. Roosevelt in the presence of Prime Minister Winston Churchill at the Quebec Conference in 1943.

9. HOLD ON.

The de-skid truck that drives the commander of the gendarmerie of the city of Meung-sur-Loire and his wife arrives after a little more than forty-five minutes of travel. It must be said that the road in those years was certainly not of good qualities as we can see nowadays. In addition, the journey in the truck was not easy. Indeed, the people in the back were not at ease. You were tossed from side to side.

The soldiers of the German army had decided that the commander of the gendarmerie of the city of Meung-sur-Loire should be taken to their building. For this reason, the truck stopped in front of the FeldKommandantur.

When they arrived, a group of soldiers came out of the building and stood around the truck. Alain, the commander of the gendarmerie wonders if he had not been denounced by a third person and that this is the reason why the men of the PPF and the German soldiers had come to the brigade of Meung-sur-Loire.

Then an officer of the Schutzstaffel and another man in a black suit came out of the building. The officer says.

—Commander... Go down with your lady. I introduce myself as SS-Obersturmführer Otto Von Himberburg and I introduce you to the officer of the Geheime Staatspolizei who is called Gestapo Hans Wilherman. We would like to speak with you and your wife Lucile if I am not mistaken. Please follow us.

The commander begins to fear for his wife. He wonders what the German police member can know about him and his activities with the resistance. Alain begins to fear that he has put his wife's life in danger. The commander has already heard of the Geheime Staatspolizei who is called Gestapo. Their interrogation techniques were the most violent there was. In himself, the commander wonders in case of interrogation how long he would last. He knows that perfectly. Even the best trained and most mentally resilient men and women at one point crack up and respond to interrogations. No one resists indefinitely. But here, the question is, will it last long enough for the members of the network to then get to safety and put their families to safety.

The two Magdunois follow the German officers. He enters the building. Then Lucile is asked to sit in the hallway. And actually her husband goes into an office.

—Commander... How are you?" said the SS Officer.

— I'm fine, thank you... But I'm a little puzzled by my presence here.

— Don't worry... This will be quickly settled... Trust me. The Gestapo officer replied.

—I don't understand. I am the commander of the gendarmerie brigade of Meung-sur-Loire, under the command of the Prefect and the Vichy government. Why am I here?

— Mr. Commander, we have received a letter from a person who says that you have contacts with people who are suspected of being among the terrorists who claim to be resistant?

— Oh yes... I see... A letter from so-called good French who denounces things that are not real under cover of anonymity. I know at the gendarmerie brigade of Meung-sur-Loire, we receive them very regularly. Besides, to be honest, I had to create a special service just for this type of mail. And that occupies two full-time gendarmes.

— You say his accusations are false?

— I have a question for you. Do you think I would jeopardize my career, my wife's safety just for people who have no education? You may not know it, but the gendarmerie is a military body. We have a habit of obeying the orders given without thinking too much.

— I understand... So you're saying this letter is a false accusation?

— Not only am I telling you! But I go further SS-Obersturmführer, I affirm. It may be a letter from a person to whom I gave almonds or interrogated after a crime committed by the author of this cloth!

— A question for you, commander. Do you know a woman named Martine Delporte?

— Yes, she is a resident of the city of Meung-sur-Loire. She resides, if I do not say stupidity, next to the station. But this I have to check. To be sure, Mr. Gestapo Officer. But why this question?

— This woman was arrested yesterday by the men of the PPF in the company of a man.

— I'll tell you one thing... I don't really like the men of the French People's Party or PPF. His men think they are gendarmes or policemen, but they have no real judicial power. And if she walks with a man, I don't see how it affects me. She is tall and widowed. So you will understand that it does not concern me.

— Yet when the men of the PPF told you to follow him, did you do it?

— Be careful, Mr. Gestapo Officer, do not extrapolate my attitude. It was not the men of the PPF that I followed, but it was the soldiers of your army. Which is not the same thing. Know, as I told you, that I have more respect for the military even if they are not French than for the men of the French People's Party.

— I see what you mean commander and I understand you. But let's go back to that woman Martine Delporte and that man who is with her, if you will. Say the SS-Obersturmführer.

— You see!

— The man in question is a British officer who has been parachuted into your area. Your wife is a great friend with this Mrs. Martine Delporte?

— So I can't tell you that. Personally, I have enough work in the gendarmerie brigade and I confess that I will not spend my time monitoring all the actions of my wife. But I know that this Martine was at school with my tender wife. So, it is more than very likely they remained on good terms as we say at home.

— Thank you for your information. On the other hand, you will stay with us a little.

The officer of the Schutzstaffel, SS-Obersturmführer Otto Von Himberburg, called a guard and told him.

— Guard! Take the commander into the waiting room and bring his wife into the office.

— At your command SS-Obersturmführer!

The guard takes the commander of the gendarmerie out of Meung-sur-Loire and directs him to a small room where his wife Lucile is. The young woman looks at her husband and tells him.

— Are you okay? What do they want from us?

— Martine and a man were arrested yesterday afternoon. And the man in question is English.

— Oh my God!

— Silence! It is forbidden to talk to each other! Besides, Madam follow me! said the guard.

A few moments later the young guard, who seemed to be in his twenties, returned to the Commander and Lucile. He pointed to the Commander's wife and told her.

— You! Please follow me! The officers want to talk to you!

The young woman gets up feverishly and follows the young German soldier to the office door where her husband was a few minutes earlier. A few seconds later, Martine passes in front of the door of the room where the Commander is, and she too goes under good escorts towards the office. Arriving at the door, Martine finds the wife of the Commander of the gendarmerie of Meung-sur-Loire. The soldier who escorted Lucile knocked on the door. A voice is heard.

—Come in!

The young soldier opened the door of the office and there the two German officers look at the two young women who do not say any words and who do not look at each other. The young soldier enters the office and stands on his side, leaving access to the two women who are waiting, hesitantly in front of the door. One of the guards of Martine's escort pushed the young woman into the office. Then the soldier returns in turn. The young soldier who had led Lucile to the room bowed his head and told her.

— Madam... Please enter!

Lucile enters the office in turn. Lucile notices that Martine has marks of a blow on her face. The wife of the Commander of the Gendarmerie begins to worry about the intention of the Officers of the German Army present in the room.

— Please sit down, ladies!... We have a few questions for you... If I may...

— These are your offices, Mr. Officer... So I don't see the reason you're asking for our permission to ask us questions...

— That's right... These are our offices, Madam Commander's wife... My sentence was how to say... A formula of politeness... You know, I'm not very good at your language...

— I personally think that you speak a rather correct French for a person who says he is not good at our language...

— Thank you for your compliment...

— SS-Obersturmführer... Just!... We are not here to make worldliness!...

— I remind you that the Geheime Staatspolizei has no order to give to the Schutzstaffel!

— They are terrorists, and you talk to them as if you were on a social evening in Berlin!

— I speak to his ladies as I please! And it's by a member of the Gestapo who will tell me how to talk to people. Know that I had a military education and like any officer we have a code of conduct. We are not former peasants who have been given an uneducated uniform!

— Ladies!... You will speak. I have very strong methods for you to tell me all what I want to know!...

— A question... A foreign army attacks your country... Will you stand by and do not act? said Martine.

— You are terrorists!

— Personally, I consider myself a patriot! But everyone has their own point of view!

— And you, Madam Wife of the Commander of the Gendarmerie... Are you a terrorist?

— Of course not! I am French!

— Are you helping this Jewish terrorist against the army of the Third Reich?

— I told you... I am French... I defend my country and its people!

— So you are helping this woman against the German army? But know that your Marshal Pétain is a patriot!

— For Marshal Pétain... That's your point of view... The old man is senile and as for defending France, he delivered it to you! I don't call it patriotism! ... Martine is my best friend... And more for information... She is not Jewish!

— Your husband is that you are a terrorist?

— We are French! And proud to be! ... And until there are Germans in our towns and villages... Our duty as French is to all the massacred! Martine replies.

— Madam Commander's wife... Don't have anything to say? ...

—Yes! ... Long live France! ... And Vive de Gaulle! ...

Following his words spoken by Lucile, the wife of the Commander of the brigade of the gendarmerie of Meung-sur-Loire, the two women, begin to sing La Marseillaise, anthem of the French Republic. They sang so loudly that from the waiting room the Commander of the gendarmerie, Alain, hears the song and accompanies it. It should be noted that at that time the German authorities did not allow the singing of the anthem of the French Republic. But the sound of patriotic singing passes through the walls and floors and is heard throughout the FeldKommandantur building. Other French people arrested by the German authorities began to sing the French national anthem. This sound of singing makes the Germans bewildered by the attitude of his few Frenchmen.

—Stop! ... This song is forbidden! ... Stop! ... Es ist Verboten!! ...

The band sings even louder. The German soldiers began to get angry and start knocking on the doors of the cells where the prisoners were. But seeing that it bothers, the German occupation troops, the detainees sing more beautifully.

— Silence! Shouts the German soldiers.

But the prisoners did not obey the orders of the German troops.

—Stop! Be quiet! the Germans are screaming.

Meanwhile, in the office where Martine and the wife of the gendarmerie commander, Lucile, are located, the head of the German political police punch Lucile. Then he turned around and hit Martine in turn. Then he told them.

— You! you're going to be silent? When we give an order, you must obey. Am I clear?

Lucile looks at the officer with a black look filled with hatred in front of this man who is most abject according to the vision of the young woman. Then she said to him in a voice of the most assertive.

— Do you feel like a man? You are so small that, to compensate for your small size, you have to hit defenseless women.

The Gestapo officer looked at the young woman and began to give her a big slap. He hit the young woman so hard that she fell from his chair. Lucile got up and spat in the German officer's face. This annoyed the head of the Gestapo more. He walked up to Lucile and punched her in the stomach. By the force of the blow, the young woman bent in half and held her belly.

— Yes, I think, you must be happy to hit women. Hey Lucile.

— Personally, I don't mind hitting a woman or a man. It comes down to the same thing. I always take so much pleasure in hitting people. Said the Gestapo officer.

The second officially present in the room, seeing this, began to scream.

— That is enough. Guard helped this young woman to sit on the seat. And you're going to escort the Gestapo officer out of the office. I don't expect this man to be in the office while I question his ladies.

The German soldier gave the military salute. Then he grabbed the Gestapo officer's arm and escorted him out of the office. The Gestapo officer did not appreciate the soldier's gesture, giving him a big blow of the shoulder. The German army officer who had given the order to take out the Gestapo official, looks at him and tells him.

— As I told you here, I am the one in charge, and I am the one who decides who is in the office and who should leave it. And know that the soldiers obey that to me, if I say that you must be outside, they obey. They do not obey, to the Gestapo, they are not agents of the Gestapo. They are soldiers.

— Your attitude is intolerable. As a Gestapo officer, I will report to my superiors. We'll see who has the last word.

— Well, make your report, you're just good at doing that. You are dishonouring the German people. And I'm not from the Gestapo, I'm from the Wehrmacht.

— I wonder if you are not with these terrorists? Against the German army and the Third Reich.

— I forbid you to say such stupidity, it will change you a little.

The soldier violently pushed the Gestapo officer out of the room. The Wehrmacht officer turned to the two women. Then he said to them in a calm and gentle voice.

— Please excuse us for the attitude of this Gestapo officer, know that we are not responsible for these acts, these words, or his thoughts. These are men who think they are police officers. As I told you. We are military. And we respect the military and civilians. But it is true that if you help terrorists, I will not be able to do anything for you. And this, this vermin knows very well.

— Mr. Officer, know that we are French patriots, and we are for our country for its freedom of thought. And his freedom to live free.

The Wehrmacht officer nodded and said.

— Know that I understand your point of view. If the situation were reversed, know that I would do the same as you. I will defend my people against their enemy.

The two women began to look at each other. Then Martine turns to the officer and tells him.

— Mr. Officer, I grant you; I am part of the resistance. Know personally that I have nothing against you. You have not personally done anything to me. But as you are told, we are patriots and therefore we defend our people and our convictions.

— But can I ask you a question please?

— If I can answer that, ask your question.

— What will happen to us?" From our families, from our friends.

— Well, how do you tell yourself?" Do you admit that you are a resistance fighter? So, under German law, you are considered a terrorist. And unfortunately, people considered terrorists have gone through arms.

— Even we women went through arms? Yet we are civilians, we have nothing military.

— No, you women are sent to Germany, to prisons. But believe me, it's worse than death. You can't even imagine what women go through in German prisons. These are horrible camps. You work, you are fed very little. And very often, you are hit. Personally, I have nothing to do with german National Socialist. I am a soldier. I am not a Nazi. But as a soldier, I have to obey the orders of my superiors. Sorry.

At that moment, Martine and Lucile understood that the officer in front of them had nothing to do with the Gestapo officer. That this man could have a good background. But that unfortunately, he had no choice. He had to do his job.

— But I don't want to go to Germany, I stay in France. Hey Lucile.

— Unfortunately, you will have no choice. That's the way it is. It is rare for the German army to execute women. On the other hand, for men, unfortunately, it is the firing squad.

— Madam, may I ask you a question, was your husband aware that you were one of the terrorists of the resistance?

— We have a fusional relationship. I never told him about the network of resistance. But I think he must have suspected it a little bit.

— That you did not talk about the network of the resistance can work in its favor.

But on the other hand, I cannot guarantee that my superiors will allow him to keep his life saved. Know that I understand your actions and your idea. But you see, my superiors sometimes fear the reactions of the German National Socialists.

— I understand, but can I see it?

— I will ask the guard to lead you into your cells. And I will give them instructions so that you can spend some time with your spouse.

— Thank you, Mr. Officer.

The officer got up and walked to the door and asked the guards to go into the office and he told them.

— Guard, please return these women to their cells. And know that I ask you to leave a few moments between the commander's wife and her husband. I allow him a one-hour visit.

The guards returned to the office. Then the guards supervised, the two women and took them out of the office. He went to the waiting room where the commander of the gendarmerie of Meung-sur-Loire was. The guards paused briefly and one of them told the commander of the gendarmerie.

— We will drive you to your cells, please follow us.

The commander looked at his wife Lucile and Martine and he understood that the two women had to speak and therefore that the Germans knew about the resistance network. He got up and followed the guards with his wife and Martine. And he walked to the stairs that lead to the cellar of the building. At that time, the head of the guards told the commanders of the gendarmerie.

— Our officer allows you to have an hour one-on-one with your wife. Enjoy this moment.

After Lucile, Martine, and the commander entered the cell, the guard closed the door behind them.

After a few minutes that the guard left the cells, Lucile tells her husband.

— The Germans know that I am a member of the resistance. But rest assured, I said you didn't know. Perhaps, it will allow you to have your life saved. The German Officer said that we would risk being sent to Germany in special camps.

— Why, did you say I didn't know? I am perfectly aware that you are part of the resistance. I remind you that I am a member of the network too.

— I didn't want you to be shot. Because this is what he expects from the men who are captured by the Germans and who are members of the resistance.

— I am tall, and I made a choice at the beginning of the war. I have chosen to defend my country, my friends, and my fellow citizens. That you say that I am not aware makes me look like a coward and that I do not want.

— But we both know that you're not a coward. I only hope that when I go to Germany, that everything will go well and that I will get back to you very soon.

After a few minutes, the guard opens the door and enters. He was followed by the Gestapo officer and the Wehrmacht officer. When they returned, the couple no longer said a single word.

— You saw that man is also a terrorist. Say the Gestapo officer.

— Mrs. Lucile, you told me that your husband was not aware of the fact that you are part of the resistance. So you lied to me?

— The duty of a wife is to protect her husband.

— How can you trust these vile and infamous rats who are terrorists?" Tell the Gestapo officer to his Wehrmacht counterpart.

— I am a man who trusts human genders.

— What foolishness to trust your people. They are all crooks, liars, and stinking rats of their so-called resistance. To a Wehrmacht officer, you seem stupid to me.

The Wehrmacht officer lowered his head. The Gestapo officer, proud of his finding and induced of his person, looks at him and tells him.

— So, we can consider the commander of the gendarmerie as a terrorist and therefore he must be considered as such and therefore he must have passed by the weapons. After all, he is a terrorist. Did I make myself understood correctly, Mr. Officer of the Wehrmacht? Of course, I am not a soldier like you, but I am not stupid like you.

The fate was sealed. The commander of the gendarmerie was to be executed the next day by the German soldiers. As for the two women, they would be transferred to a prisoners' camp in Germany.

— Guard, close the door behind us and make sure he is well monitored, because they are terrorists.

After the two officers left the cell, the soldier closed the door.

As the hours passed, the commander began to go around in circles in the cell. His wife Lucile had fallen asleep. He watched her sleep sadly. Martine looked at him and said.

— I don't know how she manages to get to sleep during such a moment.

— It's simple, she does as my mother always taught me. We, when we want to sleep at all costs, we can't do it. But when you want to stay awake, that's where you fall asleep.

The commander stopped talking for a short time. Then he continued his sentence.

— Martine, did you know my mother was a nurse?

— No, I didn't know, Alain.

— My mother was a nurse and she worked at night. I loved talking to my mother when she came home from work in the early morning. But very often, I pretended to sleep when she came home it reassured her. My mother, usually standing in the door frame to watch me sleep. And I closed my eyes. I didn't want her to be sad to see her child waiting for her to come home so she could talk to him. But you know what's the saddest, Martine? It's that sometimes I tried to stay awake to talk with my mother. I wanted so much to be able to talk to him when he arrived from work. Unfortunately, I was falling asleep. That's when I understood. When you want to stay awake, you have to want to sleep. And when you want to fall asleep, you have to want to stay awake.

— I didn't know. Is your mother still alive Alain?

— No, she is dead. And fortunately. Because she would not have liked to see the France under German occupation.

— I'm sorry. It's all my fault. If I hadn't convinced you and your wife to join the resistance, Lucile'd have her life saved.

— Know that this is my idea. Even if you hadn't been in the resistance, know that I would have been part of the resistance.

— Do you think it's going to be like tomorrow, Alain?

— It's simple, they'll pick us up. Getting us into trucks. You will go to Germany in the camps. And I'm going towards my destiny. Can I ask you to watch over my wife when you are there in Germany?

Martine did not have time to answer Alain's question. In the corridors, the sounds of boots were heard. This noise so characteristic of the boots of the German soldiers. Then they heard a key, tucked into the lock of the cell door. The door opened. And guards returned to the cell. The most senior of the guards, said.

— Please stand up and follow us. We have to leave. It's time.

The commander of the gendarmerie woke up his wife and told her to get up and come with him and Martine. The small group climbed the stairs which leads them into the central courtyard of the building. There, parked in the courtyard of the building, three trucks were waiting for them with the engine on. In each truck, armed German soldiers were already seated. The soldiers push the prisoners towards the trucks. And each in turn, he climbs the small steps to climb to the back of the truck. Second Lieutenant Billing was already present in the truck. Then the trucks made their way to their destination.

10. GOODBYE FRANCE!

The vehicles are heading west of Orleans. After about thirty minutes, the trucks enter some wood. They embark on a forest road. The forest road is so bad that the people in the back of the truck, at each of the holes fell from their seats. Martine was sitting right next to the entrance to the back door and a guard is facing her. Throughout the journey, Martine looks outside. She wishes to mark in her mind the image of the France and her childhood region. Second Lieutenant Billing was placed three places away. The young officer observed the young woman. Martine looked at him and gave him a smile. All of a sudden, Martine jumped through the opening of the back of the truck. The two guards who were supposed to be watching her were surprised by the young woman's attitude. Both stand up. They arm their machine guns and shoot Martine. Just as the two German soldiers who had custody of Martine fired, Lieutenant Billing stood up. But the soldiers who watch him immediately put him in play. One of the soldiers told him.

— In your place, I would not attempt anything.

Billing raises his hands in the air. Then he said.

— I'm not crazy, I'm not trying to escape.

At the time of the explosion of the machine guns, the truck stopped. And of all the trucks, the soldiers were going out to see what had happened. One of the officers who were in the convoy came to the back of the convoy to see what had happened. It advances towards Martine's inert body. And with his foot, he turned the body upside down. Seeing that the young woman was dead. The German officer took out his pistol and shot her in the head. Then he goes back to the truck where Martine was, and he says in a firm voice.

— This woman is stupid, she wanted to escape, but the guards were ordered to shoot if you try to escape. So, remember this, if you want to escape. You will be killed. And it will be without warning. Did I make myself understood?

The prisoners inside the truck or, to be Martine, understood that the German soldiers were not laughing. Alain looked at his wife Lucile with a tender look filled with love for his young wife. Then he looked at Martine's inert body. From this body bruised by the bullets of the German soldiers, one could see a pool of red-scarlet blood spread out on the gravel road of the forest. The young wife of the gendarmerie commander, Lucile, when she saw the inert and lifeless body of her childhood friend, felt tears in her eyes and she began to cry. Because the latter knew the fate that was reserved for her husband. She knew that the next time the trucks stopped, it would be to drive her sweet husband to death. A few moments later, the convoy of death resumes its journey to its fateful destination.

Ten minutes have passed since the last stop. The convoy stopped. And the soldiers start screaming in German.
—Let all the men get off the truck and line up next to each other.

The soldiers get all the men off the truck, Commander Alain, and Second Lieutenant Billing. With the latter, there were about twenty other people. The youngest must have been just fifteen years old, but he was already promised certain death and programmed by the German troops.

Lucile looks at the young child just out of childhood. One could see in the child's eyes the fear of dying. The young boy, whom Lucile did not know, made him remember Lucien. The young boy, who died in the offices of the French Populist Party.

Once the men were aligned, the German soldiers advanced them towards the undergrowth. In the undergrowth, a trench was dug a few days earlier. The German soldiers ordered the men to enter the trench and advance towards the end of the trench. Once, the first man arrived at the end of the trench. The Germans give them the signal to stop. At the same time, a vehicle reversed and stopped a few meters from the prisoners. A tarpaulin stood up. And at that moment, the prisoners could see a machine gun positioned and ready to fire. The officer moved and placed himself next to the truck where the machine gun was located. And once loud and clear, he says.
— Army... We play... Fire...

At the moment when the officer gave the last order ordering the execution of the prisoners. Several prisoners start screaming.
— Long live France!
— Long live de Gaulle!
— For King George VI! Say Billing.

On the last words of the British officer, the sound of the machine gun breaks the silence of the forest in the early morning. The German officer approached each of the men who were lying on the ground, took out his weapon and fired a bullet into each of the prisoners' heads. The last to receive the bullet fired by the German officer is the young boy whom Lucile contemplates with sadness.

A few minutes later, the German soldiers returned to the truck. The engines of the vehicles begin to roar. Then the trucks left for Germany. Inside one of the trucks is Lucile the wife of the commander who had just been executed with Second Lieutenant Billing, but also a dozen other women.

Meanwhile, Cédric, Lauren, Laurent, and Isaac managed to make our way towards Vierzon. The town of Vierzon was the place where the closest demarcation line to Orléans is located. It is through this city that the small group decided to move to the free zone. A day earlier, Cedric had given instructions to the group of British and Belgian soldiers who were in the hideout of Epieds-en-Beauce to go towards Vierzon. When the small group of four arrived, he was reunited with the other British and Belgian soldiers. A group of local resistance fighters, welcome them and hide them. A few days later, they will have to cross the demarcation line to find themselves in free land. Cédric knew the head of the local network perfectly because it is his brother Mathieu.

Mathieu was happy to see his little brother again despite the fact that he would have preferred to find him in other circumstances. Cédric, before leaving, had managed to recover Lieutenant Billing's notebook that Adrien gave him. In this notebook, one could find information that the British officer, Second Lieutenant Billing, had managed to collect before being arrested by the men of the PPF. Once in the free zone, the small group knew that they should not relax their attention in the face of the PPF men who were also in this area. It should be noted that in France at that time, it was not only in the occupied area that there were men of the PPF. Inveterate collaborator with the Germans, but also in the free zone. But you could also find militiamen there. The militiamen were Vichy's auxiliary police force and it wreaked havoc on the abusive population, sometimes beating and killing people because they did not support the German occupation of French territory.

— When we spent free zone? Cedric asks his brother.

— The safest thing is that you have to

pass tomorrow. You should rest because you are going to have to get up from very early to four o'clock.

— We will be ready. Don't worry. Answer Cédric.

— And what we do for Lieutenant Billing and Martine. Lauren asks.

— Unfortunately, I am afraid I have bad news for you. According to the information we received from Orleans. They were transported into the woods where the Germans execute people. But usually, women are taken to Germany in camps. Mathieu explains.

— You mean Lieutenant Billing is dead?" Lauren asks.

— Indeed. Lieutenant Billing must be dead today. But it wasn't just him. The Germans executed many people that day. And we know from reliable sources that a woman was killed. Among the men we knew was Alain.

— How is Alain among the victims? Ask Cédric.

— This information does not come from me; it comes from Orleans. The day you left Martine's house. The Germans went to the gendarmerie, and we boarded with his wife.

— His German rats killed, Alain, and you tell me that now. And Lucile? You told me that there was a woman who had died.

— For Lucile, I don't know, I only know

that there is a woman who has died, we have not been told her identity. But according to the description, it would be more a woman who would look like Martine.

— Are you sure?

— I told you I don't know. But according to the description that the network gave us, it would be Martine. We didn't manage to get there in time, we couldn't save anyone.

Cedric gives a big slap in a glass of water that was on the table. The glass broke against the wall. Suddenly, this announcement made by Mathieu threw a cold throughout the room. Cédric keeps busy for a period of time. Then he said.

— I'm going back to Orléans, I want to know.

— But you're completely crazy, brother. If one of them has spoken, you will be sought after by your colleagues. And that would be too dangerous for the entire network.

— Martine, Lucile, and Alain helped a lot of people. We need to know exactly what happened. And to know who betrayed us.

— Because you think it was a leak within the network that made them denounced?

— I don't know, I'm not in the office so I can't get the information. But there is definitely a leak somewhere. We have to find it in order to eliminate it.

The arrest of Martine, Lucile and Alain makes the network fear that the group has been infiltrated by a sleeping agent of the Germans. Cedric wanted to know at all costs who had betrayed their friends. He had to find the mole so that he could eliminate it and to be able to act freely. It should be noted that at that time, many resistance networks were infiltrated by German sleeper agents. Many networks have been betrayed by the French. Who worked for the Germans or for the Vichy militia. Many brave resistance fighters died through their own fault. Lauren was sad to hear that good and so-called French betray their own compatriots for the Germans. She looked at Cedric and told him.

— I will come with you. I will help you.

— No, it's far too dangerous for you. It is better that you go to the free zone and return to England with as much information as possible to be able to drive the Germans out of my country.

— I would point out that the Germans killed my superior, Lieutenant Billing. What will I be able to say in London when we go back?

— Well, you will tell them that he died as a hero, that he died for his ideas and his country. And that thanks to him, we were able to collect some information to help the resistance recover France.

— I should have gone in his place.

— Yes, today you would either be dead or in a prison camp in Germany.

Laurent turns to Lauren and tells her.
— Cedric is absolutely right; you would be in a camp in Germany today. Worse, you would be dead. Our duty is to inform London as the orders we have received. I know, Lauren, you're not a soldier, but orders are orders.
— Yes, but sometimes these orders are stupid. Through our negligence, Lieutenant Billing died.
— You didn't do any negligence Lauren. Lieutenant Billing is a career soldier and that's exactly what he expected. He knew he could die during this operation. But his duty as a soldier outweighed his decision. And he preferred to give his life to save the lives of others. And that, the France can never forget. Especially me. Hey Laurent.

The evening began. Cedric looks out the window. Isaac, Lauren's older brother, comes to meet her. He was looking at Cedric for a few moments. And he said to her.
— Cédric, you seem to me to be a good man. You have high ideas. And sometimes I can tell you that I share them. But most of all, I wanted to thank you for telling Lauren to stay. It would be horrible for me if I lost it. You

understand? She's my little sister. And I can't even imagine her condition when she discovered the death of our parents.

— I understand you; I also appreciate Lauren. And I'm sorry for your parents.

— Don't be sorry, you have nothing to do with it. It's the Germans. What can I hate Germans! They made people suffer so much. You know, the children who were with us? Simon explained to me that he saw the death of his parents. There, right in front of his eyes. This was when they were evacuating from Belgium to escape the advance of German troops.

— So I didn't know what had happened to Simon and his parents. I only knew he had no one. That he was alone.

— He wasn't alone, he had his friends and there were us. When he said he was going to accompany Lieutenant Billing and Martine, I thought he was very brave.

— I confess that I too found him very courageous. And I'm sad that he died.

— He had decided, and no one could change his mind.

— That's right, he looked pretty stubborn.

— You can't even imagine. You know, I feel like my little sister Lauren appreciates you very much.

— I also appreciate her very much, that's

why she must not come with me. It's too risky and I don't want anything to happen to him.

— Me neither, but I know she would have been safe with you.

Cedric smiles at Isaac. That night, everything was so quiet. Members of the resistance had placed themselves in guard posts in several places around the building where the small group was taking refuge. Cedric was going to leave early the next morning. Lauren prepared food for him so he could last a few days. It was around five thirty in the morning that Cédric took the vehicle and left for Orleans. Before leaving, he wanted to stay for a few moments with each of the people present in the house. He was getting a little longer with Lauren. And he said to her in a sad voice.

— Pay attention to yourself. If there is the least danger, run.

— It's not up to us to pay attention. We are close to the free zone, it is up to you, you return to the zone occupied by the German soldiers.

— I know how to do particularly well. And I still have my police card, so just in case... I could take it out. It's easier for me as a police officer to pass the checks. That you, it may be dangerous.

— If Martine, Lucile, or Alain have spoken, you may be sought after by your colleagues. So, please pay attention to yourself.

— Don't worry, I'll be very careful. And I hope to see you again one day.

— Me too. Good luck.

— Good luck to you.

Cédric gets in the traction and makes his way towards Orleans. Lauren watches him leave. Then she turns around. Isaac, Lauren's older brother, noticed that her younger sister was crying. Isaac walks up to her and has taken her in his arms. Mathieu, Cédric's younger brother, joins them. And their sayings.

— I'm sorry to bother you, but we have to leave. We must cross the border between the occupied zone and the free zone before the German patrols pass.

— We are coming. Hey Lauren.

Cédric's little brother, Mathieu, had decided that the group would be divided into four small groups. The groups would be composed of British soldiers, Belgian soldiers and five members of the local resistance. Mathieu had decided that he would be in Lauren, Isaac, and Laurent's group. Small groups for more safety would go through different paths. But all of them were going to end up in the free zone in the same place. A small farm known to Cédric and Mathieu. Mathieu estimated the travel time for each group of about twenty-five minutes. The start was also going to happen by shifting for each of the groups. A first group composed of five British, two Belgians and five resistance fighters set off as scouts. About eight minutes later, it is the group of Lauren, Mathieu, Isaac, Laurent two British soldiers and a Belgian to set out towards the demarcation line.

— Be careful if you hear anything, let me know. It can be a group of German soldiers.

—Yes, we will be very careful.

The group had decided to go through a small forest to be able to return to the free zone. They tried to walk as discreetly as possible. But because they were moving forward quietly, it makes them take much longer than expected. In the distance, you could hear dogs barking. But what reassured the group was that orders were not heard shouting in German. He continues to move forward, slowly, but surely, towards freedom. During this journey, Lauren wonders where Cedric was. Has he ever arrived in Orleans? Did he reach his destination safe and sound? Will she have any news? These questions loop all the time in his head. Lauren would have appreciated it, accompanied Cédric. After a long walk, Mathieu asks them.

— You saw his poles with the barbed wire above?

— Yes, I saw why?" Isaac asks.

— Well, that's because that's where we're going to go. This is called the dividing line between the occupied zone and the free zone.

— And how are we going to get through? Are we going to go above or below? Lauren asks.

— Why do you want to go above or below? We will simply cut the wire mesh to get through.

—Oh yes, it's much simpler. But you don't fear that this will be visible?

— No... Rest assured here, in our region, there is a lot of big game. The Germans still think that it is the wild boars that destroy their fences. The day after tomorrow or a few days later, there will be a German engineering team that will be there. And they will simply replace the wire mesh.

— Ah, okay, he really thinks they're wild boars?"

— You know, Germans aren't always very smart. Mathieu explains.

— Yes, but he should still realize that they are not wild boars.

— As I told you, not all Germans are intelligent. Sometimes I even wonder if they had ever seen wild boars before coming here? And you know, wild boars, it's a lot of damage. Hey Mathieu.

— I think there must be wild boars in Germany. Lauren replies.

— I can't tell you; I've never been to

Germany. Answer Mathieu.

— And you're not afraid that a patrol will arrive as we pass? Laurent asks.

— We just have to be careful. Stanislas, Damien, go see if the passage is free. Take the pliers to cut the wire mesh.

Stanislas and Damien moved forward discreetly to open the passage. The two men on the last meters begin to crawl on the ground to be able to reach the fence in all discretion. Then Stanislaus got up and began to cut the fence. Meanwhile, Damien was on his knees to watch the area. Once the fence is cut, Stanislas kneels to monitor the area in turn. Damien signals to Mathieu that the group must move forward to cross the line. The rest of the group began to advance towards the fence, but with their backs bent to be as little visible as possible. One by one, all the members of the team pass the fence. Once on the other side, they return together to the undergrowth that was not far away. They were finally in the free zone. Mathieu gathers the small group around him to talk to them.

—That's it, we are finally in the free zone, but be careful. Here there are also militiamen and men from the French People's Party. And believe me they are not tender.

— We know, we have a young friend. A young boy, I mean. Who was killed by his men from the French People's Party. Lauren replies.

— Well, that's not the whole thing, but we still have a little bit of roads. So forward.

The group advances to a large farm. They enter the courtyard. And Mathieu directs them directly to a part of a building. He opens the door. And in this building is the first group that had left a little before Mathieu's group. Mathieu went to see a young woman who is next to the group already installed and who gives them something to eat. Mathieu looks at her and tells her.

— Benedict, we have arrived. While we were in Vierzon, we had a communication. This is your sister. Based on the descriptions we have received. The Germans would have executed him.

The young woman dropped her pan. Then she fell to her knees on the ground. And starts crying while screaming.

— No... What for? But why?

The group that had just arrived immediately understood that it was Martine's sister. Seeing her, Lauren finds that there is an air of resemblance to Martine. The sad thing for Lauren is that this woman's sister is dead. For a mission she was not trained for. But Lauren thinks of Martine's son. Martine's son was in the third group that was to join the free zone. For greater security, only Belgian soldiers and resistance fighters were with the young boy. The third group had to go by road. Among the resistance fighters of this group are several gendarmes. So they have a lot more faculties to go through the road. In case of control, they can say that they are accompanying the child to an orphanage. Bénédicte, Martine's sister, asks Mathieu.

— And my godson, Mathieu, my sister's son where is he?

— Don't worry, your godson will arrive in not long. He was not in our group; he is in the third group. It should not be long in coming.

No sooner had he finished this sentence than the young boy entered the building. The young man starts running towards his godmother and aunt.

— Tata Benedict... I'm glad to see your aunt. I was told I was coming to see you. But a question, mom has already arrived?

— No, she's not here, my favorite nephew. I am sorry.

The young woman cannot hold back her sobs. She thought of her sister whom the Germans had killed.

— Why are you crying tata? said the young boy.

— I cry for nothing. I just never feared

seeing you again.

Seeing this scene, Lauren thinks of her parents whom she had found dead in Finchley in the north suburbs of London. She, too, thought she would never find her brother, who for her at the beginning of the war, was considered dead in battle. The young woman lets tears flow. She thought back to the moment of spending with Martine. The dress and perfume that Martine had offered there. She hadn't known Martine much, but she knew that the young woman was a person with a big heart. Martine had not hesitated to hide them when they arrived in France. And this even at the risk of his life and that of his child. Benedict takes a fork, a knife and a plate and feeds her nephew. When Benedicte walked away from the child Lauren, approached to talk to him.

— Hello, excuse me for bothering you. I know the timing is wrong, but I'm guessing you're Martine's sister.

—That was correct. Martine was my sister; she was my big sister.

— First of all, let me express our deepest condolences. Martine was a great woman. She did not hesitate to help us. The moment we were parachuted. She did not hesitate to hide us in her cellar.

— I recognize my sister's state of mind. But why were you parachuted?

— We are from England, and we were parachuted by order of London.

— You're not French?

— No, personally, I am British and so is my brother. But he was already in France before I arrived. Finally, he was on the side of Dunkirk at the beginning of the war. But before the British troops were surrounded at Dunkirk, they managed to escape. And they were hidden in a hiding place in Epieds-en-Beauce.

— We are from a family of patriots, and we always defend people. Especially against the Germans.

— Your sister gave me at the beginning of our presence a dress and perfume if you want, I give them back to you.

— No, it was my sister who gave them to you. If she gave them to you. She gave them to you. It is not done to return a gift that has been given to you. Even if the person is dead. You know what I mean?

— I understand, but it was so that you would have a memory of her.

— The memory I will have of her is through her son. And my duty as a godmother is to explain to her what her mother did. And the reason for his death. He must know that his mother had convictions. And for his convictions, to give her life to save others.

— You will be able to tell her that thanks

to her, all those who are present here today have been saved. And who must always be proud of his mother.

— Don't worry, I'll tell him when he's a little older.

At this point in the conversation between the two women, Mathieu approaches and says.

— Lauren, you would have to ask your radio operator if they could get the message to London to ask you to evacuate. I entrust you with the notebook that my brother gave me. It should be handed over to your superiors in England. We think this could be important for your superiors.

—Very good. I will inform Laurent right away. But why do you come and ask me to talk to him? Laurent speaks French. And I am not his superior. It was Lieutenant Billing, his superior.

— From what I understand Laurent, listen to you as if they were orders, so I thought you were his superior.

—Certainly not. He's been in the military longer than I have. I have been in the army since June.

Lauren goes to see Laurent to tell him to pass on the information to London to try to evacuate the people present on the farm. Laurent takes the briefcase where the radio is located and installs it on the table. He begins to transmit the information that Mathieu asks him to transmit to London. A few hours later, he received a message from London informing them that they were going to evacuate the entire group. The evacuation was scheduled for three days later. Lauren in her heart hopes that Cedric comes back to see her before she leaves. But unfortunately, Cedric was busy in Orleans.

The day of departure arrives. Members of the local resistance had marked the landing place of the plane and secured the area. A plane arrives and lands on the ground. A side door opens, and a man starts screaming.

— Come on, hurry. Quickly... Quickly... Quickly...

British and Belgian soldiers rush in, along with Lauren, her brother Isaac and Laurent. After getting on the plane, Lauren before closing the door, looks one last time at France. And she thinks of Cedric, who remains in France.

After several hours of flight, the plane landed near London. British and Belgian soldiers get off the plane and are taken by security officers into a building in interrogation rooms. The intelligence officers wanted to know if among these soldiers there no German spies were. Lieutenant O'Connor meets Lauren, Laurent, and his brother Isaac. He looked and told them.

— A very good return to London. I learned what had happened with Lieutenant Billing. I personally wrote to his family. Lieutenant Billing was a very good officer and also, I do not hide him, a friend.

— We're sorry, my lieutenant. We were unable to retrieve the body to bring it back with us.

— Yes, I understand that. It surprises me that the Germans have entrusted it if you have asked for it.

— On the other hand, one of the children who was with him in the mission managed to bring us a notebook. It was Lieutenant Billing who entrusted him before being captured. He noted in this notebook the various German troops he met in the vicinity of Orleans.

— It will be extremely useful to us. But I am sure that, knowing him, he must have given the Germans a hard time when they wanted to question him. He has a lot of sarcastic humor. We tended to say between officers, when one of us made a joke quite sophomoric, that he had the humor Billing. Well, on that rest. Tomorrow, I want to see you at noon, for a debriefing.

— At your command, my lieutenant. The three soldiers answer in their hearts.

Lauren, Laurent, and Isaac leave to rest.

The next day at noon, as planned by the lieutenant, they all meet at the Lieutenant's office. The lieutenant told them.

— The information transmitted in the booklet has been more than very interesting. Currently in Orleans, there would be two panzer divisions and three artillery divisions. All of you have done a remarkable job.

The lieutenant turns to Laurent and tells him.

— Radio operator, Corporal Laurent, you have done a remarkable job, you have on meet the expectations of London. And you managed to transmit the data so that we have it as quickly as possible.

— Thank you, my Lieutenant. Answer Laurent.

— Sergeant Isaac. You have shown great courage, you have managed to get through France. Finally, much of France. And you managed to avoid the encirclement in Dunkirk for you and some of your Belgian comrades and allies.

— A very big thank you my Lieutenant.

Then Lieutenant O'Connor turned to Lorraine. He smiled wide and said to her.

— Lauren... Lauren... Lauren... You know, when Lieutenant Billing appointed you for this mission, I thought we were going straight into the wall. Well, you managed to prove me wrong. And I admit it, in front of you, I was wrong. Lieutenant Billing was right to trust you. In your abilities. And about your sharp mind. Even if you weren't on the goal that was originally planned. All of you have managed to change your goal and collect essential information. And I want to thank you all. Now you can go home, you have at least a week of vacation. After that, you have to come back to work. The war is not over. It has only just begun.

— Thank you, my lieutenant.

— Lauren, enjoy your brother's return.

— Absolutely my lieutenant.

Lauren, Isaac, and Laurent leave the Lieutenant's office. Laurent shakes Isaac's hand. And he kisses Lauren. And he tells them.

— I was delighted to meet you, Isaac. Lauren, I enjoyed being on your team. Who knows, maybe we'll find ourselves in a next mission? I will go back to see my wife and child. They must be worried.

— I, too, was delighted to meet you with Corporal Laurent. For a Frenchman, are you pretty fun? said Isaac.

— I didn't know you never said you were married, and you also had a child. Hey Lauren.

— You know, we didn't have much time to talk. We were too busy fulfilling our mission. Which is normal. I'm sorry, but I have to go. I am

in too much of a hurry to see my son again.
— See you next time. Hey Laurent.

Lauren and her brother Isaac left for London. No longer having a place of residence. And will decide to rent a small room on the south side of London. But as requested by the Lieutenant a week later, they returned to Ashford's camp.

PORTRAIT OF PEOPLE.

Lauren Elisabeth Cohan

Lauren after her return to England continued to participate in intelligence against German troops and those until the end of the war. After Adolf Hitler's victory over Germany in May 1945, a person from his past made an appearance in his life. In June 1947, she married Cédric, the French policeman she had met in Meung-Sur-Loire. She took up the profession of teacher and had five children (three girls and two boys). She named her eldest daughter by the name of Martine and her second Lucile. Her first son by the name of Nigel, her second son bears the name of Lucien and her third Alain by giving his first names to his children, she wants never to forget the people who died for the freedom of others. Lauren died at the age of 86 in 2002.

Solomon Isaiah Rosemblum called "Lucian"

Salomon was born on 13 June 1927 in Brussels (Belgium) and died on 14 March 1941 in Orléans (France) in office 210 of the French People's Party (PPF) Rue de la Bretonnerie. He was a young boy who had become an orphan following the death of both his parents during the great exodus of June 1940. The young boy resisted as best as possible in the face of the torture of the PPF interrogations. At the time of his death, Solomon was only 13 years old.

Martine Louisette Delporte says "the landlady"

Martine Louisette Delporte was born on February 12, 1913, in Orléans (France) and died on March 17, 1941, while trying to escape while she was to be transported to a camp in Germany, by German soldiers. Martine blamed herself for the death of young Lucien. His son, Lucas, will be hidden until the end of the war by friends of the resistance. Lucas will attend the trial of the person responsible for the death of young Lucien and the man who handed over his mother to the soldiers of the German army. We will never be if there was an aedile between Martine and Second Lieutenant Billing.

Nigel Édouard Billing

Nigel Édouard Billing was born on 10 January 1906 in London (England) and died on 17 March 1941 under the bullets of the German firing squad in a forest near the city of Orleans. Nigel Billing was appointed shortly before the start of the war to the rank of second lieutenant. He returned to the intelligence services of the British armies because he had a great and well-developed knowledge of Goethe's language.

Cédric Nathanaël Jean

Cédric Nathanaël Jean continued his work in the police and in the resistance. In March 1942, he was transferred to Paris. On July 13, 1942, when he had the information of the roundup of the Vel' d'Hiv for the date of July 16. Together with a group of resistance policemen, they went to inform members of the Jewish community in Paris to hide. Of the 90 people Cedric warned of the raid alone, 5 people were arrested. In July 1945, he left the police and decided to go to England with the hope of seeing Lauren again. He married Lauren on June 28, 1947. He died in 1990.

Isaac David Cohan

Isaac David Cohan returned to England with his younger sister Lauren. He participated in the Dieppe landing attempt, which was called " Jubilee" on August 19, 1942. It was a real carnage. This operation had mobilized 250 landing craft, 8,000 men, 74 squadrons of fighters and bombers. But Isaac Cohan received a burst of bullet in the heart area. He died at 11:35 a.m. on a street near the port of Dieppe where the attempted landing took place. He was 31 years old.

ABOUT THE AUTHOR

Born in France, on June 28, LE GRASSE Roger-Pierre has a real passion for history. Certain period of the past is like an attraction for him. The period of the Second World War is one among which he likes to travel.

"History is a whole that sometimes determines the future of a nation. It is through the mistakes of the past that a nation, if it understands its mistakes, can try to improve itself to avoid repeating its mistakes. No being is perfect and cannot make mistakes. All of them are the people, who must understand that mistakes must not happen again. Otherwise very quickly it can become an endless circle.

In the past of mankind, the mistakes of a people, believing in the words of a man and his friends, have led the world into a war that has unfortunately cost far too many lives. Unfortunately sometimes I wonder if humanity thinks of remembering the mistakes it has made. And what I fear is that the past will go on a loop. And that dark periods as the world experienced during the Second World War are resurfacing.

Let politicians exploit their populations as Adolf Hitler and the Nazi leaders did from their elections in 1933 until the end of their regimes in May 1945!

Unfortunately, it seems that the world has not yet understood its mistakes. »

SOME REFERENCE

Illustration

Page 37: Google My Maps satellite image of North London (England) with indication of the city of Finchley.
© Google LLC

Page 61: Google My Maps satellite image of Southeast England with indication of the city of Ashford.
© Google LLC

Page 87: Google My Maps satellite image of the region of Loiret (France) with indication of the cities of Orléans and Meung-Sur-Loire and the commune of Epieds-en-Beauce.
© Google LLC

Pages 115, 1147 and 171: Images free of commercial law and publishing.

Pages 193 and 217: © Wikipedia, a subsidiary of the Wikimedia Foundation.